# CLEO'S RAGE

DEVIL'S RIOT MC SERIES BOOK 4

E.C. LAND

DARK & DAMAGED ROMANCE PUBLISHING

# CONTENTS

Acknowledgments vii
Warning xi
Playlist xiii
Find Your Strength xv

Prologue 1
Chapter 1 5
Chapter 2 9
Chapter 3 14
Chapter 4 19
Chapter 5 24
Chapter 6 31
Chapter 7 35
Chapter 8 40
Chapter 9 45
Chapter 10 53
Chapter 11 60
Chapter 12 65
Chapter 13 71
Chapter 14 75
Chapter 15 80
Chapter 16 86
Chapter 17 91
Chapter 18 96
Chapter 19 100
Chapter 20 105
Chapter 21 110
Chapter 22 114
Chapter 23 120
Chapter 24 127
Chapter 25 131
Chapter 26 137
Chapter 27 141
Chapter 28 146
Chapter 29 153
Chapter 30 158

Chapter 31 162
Chapter 32 166
Chapter 33 170
Chapter 34 175
Epilogue 179

Social Media Links 183
Also by E.C. Land 185
Sneak Peak 191

Cleo's Rage



Publisher: Dark & Damaged Romance Publishing

Cover Design by Charli Childs, Cosmic Letterz Cover Design

Developmental Editing by Courtney Lynn Rose

Formatting by E.C. Land

Proofreading by Rebecca Vazquez

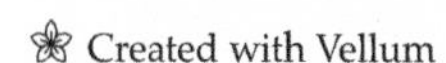

# ACKNOWLEDGMENTS

There are so many people who deserve credit in this story. My kiddos are a few of them. They love getting involved with my creative ideas and helping me bring plots together. Alongside them, I'd like to thank not only my publisher, Knox Publishing, my editor, Courtney Lynn Rose, and beta team, but I'd like to thank all of my readers who have been encouraging me as I make my way throughout this journey. You're all absolutely amazing.

*Cleo's Rage is dedicated to those who have suffered some form of self-doubt as well as those who are unable to carry life. Just remember, you're not alone and there's always a child out there waiting for you to have them with open arms.*

*You're all beautiful inside and out. Don't let anyone tell you otherwise.*

# WARNING

This content is intended for mature audiences only. It contains material that may be viewed as offensive to some readers, including graphic language, dangerous and sexual situations, murder, rape, and extreme violence.

# PLAYLIST

Home – Tyler Wood
Hurricane – Theory of a Deadman
Better than Me – Hinder
Torn to Pieces – Pop Evil
Blurry – Puddle of Mudd
Beautiful – Pop Evil
Angel's Son – Sevendust
Without You – Hinder
Angel – Theory of a Deadman
Sorry – Buckcherry
Changes – Def Tones
Coming Undone – Korn
She's My Kind of Rain – Tim McGraw
She's Still Riding Shotgun – Tyler Wood
Tell Me You Love Me – Demi Lovato
Ride – Chase Rice
Every Little Thing – Carl Pearce

# FIND YOUR STRENGTH

Look in the mirror
What do you see
Can you see yourself
Or do you see someone else
Are you as broken within as much you feel
How does one fix what can't be seen
We must find our strength from within
Pull ourselves from this slump
The pain burns within
Fire fills our veins
Consumes our bodies
Why is it so hard to feel more than doubt
Look at your self in the mirror
Say the words aloud
You're beautiful in and out
With or without anyone by your side
We can all bleed the same
Find the strength to get through the day
Let those words take over the past
We are all strong in our own way

Lean on each other to fill the void
Strength from within
That's what we all need
-E.C. Land

# PROLOGUE

## RAGE

The first time I laid eyes on Cleo, I knew I had to have her. I watched her the entire night when we first got to Franklin. I couldn't help but want to run my hands along her body. She had curves in all the right places with legs that I wanted wrapped around me as I sunk my dick in that tight pussy. Not only did I want her body but something inside told me she was meant to be mine.

That same night we met, I couldn't get enough of her. With her being a waitress at Outlaw Racks, we kept shit just between us. I didn't like it, but it was her request. By day, we were friends; by night, we fucked each other's brains out. Especially when her roommate and best friend, Lynsdey, moved out. I know it upset Cleo, but she didn't say anything about it.

Then all the shit went down with Jake, the sadistic asshole that kidnapped Lynsdey from the hospital not long after having an emergency c-section. Thorn went ballistic at having his woman taken. At the same time, we found out Cleo was missing as well. It gutted me to find out that Jake had her too.

What really got to me was when Gadget told us Jake was

raping Cleo on some website. I couldn't stop the bile from rising in the back of my throat. The knowledge of Cleo going through that sent me spiraling into a time I'd like to forget. A time where I lost my own fuckin' sister to a monster that raped and tortured her for hours before the club found her.

After all that, she ended up killing herself to escape the pain. I never really understood it until recently. My mom and dad were devastated. Hell, we all were. She was my sister for fuck's sake. Even though it was years ago, I still have a hard time dealing with it some days. However, now I get why she did it. For the same reason, Cleo attempted to do the same.

Doesn't help that after we got both girls back, I walked away from Cleo, refusing to even go into her room. I couldn't bear to see all the pain she was in. Not when she was full of spark before. So instead, I walked the fuck away. I didn't want to lose another person like that again.

Maybe if I'd gone in her room, she wouldn't have had a chance to even try to take her own life. I'll be forever thankful to Stoney for that one. No one was supposed to tell me about that shit, and it pissed me off. It wasn't until my mom called me, ripping me a new asshole that I found out during her rant. I fuckin' lost it, and that's when I realized I needed to get my shit in gear and bring my woman home.

I need to play this the right way, especially when I go to bring her ass back. I'd been paying the rent at her old place even though she wasn't there, her stuff, however, was. I refused to let anyone in there to pack her shit up. But today, I am moving her things into the house I recently purchased not far from Thorn's place. Wanting her to feel as close to the girls as she could without having to see them if she didn't want to.

Usually, I'd have gotten a prospect to move all this shit, but I just wasn't ready to have anyone else touch her stuff. Call me a pussy, I don't give a fuck, but I didn't want her shit tainted by anyone else. I want her to know when she gets back that the only one who touched anything of hers was me.

After I got everything moved, I went to talk to my prez, Twister, out of respect. I didn't want to just take off without letting him know where I'm going. I should've known he'd tell me not to go alone. We're at war now with the Dragons Fire MC. None of us should be left on the road with those crazy fuckers out there. Who knows what they're up to. They've caused a shit load of trouble recently between what all went down with Izzy and makin' a play for the docks we use.

Which brings me to now.

I shake my head to clear all the thoughts of what all went down as I ride. With me, my two brothers Hades and Burner ride along as we make our way to the national charter.

I take in a deep breath, smelling the fresh air as the wind whips around me. A calm I haven't felt in a long time hits me—I'm riding to get my woman. It's time to bring her back where she belongs.

"I'm comin' for you, Cleo. I fucked up once by walking away. This time around, we're doing things right," I murmur to myself as I hit the throttle.

# CHAPTER **ONE**

## CLEO

There's a saying that you don't know someone unless you walk a mile in their shoes. I can attest to this being true. People think they know me as a person but in all honestly, no one really knows the real me, not even my best friend Lynsdey.

Several months ago, we were taken by Lynsdey's psycho stepbrother Jake, who continuously raped me. He didn't just rape me, he humiliated me by doing it in front of her, claiming it was her punishment. How the hell does that work? I'm not some form of a whipping boy! I'm a grown-ass woman. I didn't deserve what he did to me. None of it. What Jake did, it didn't just break me physically, he crushed me mentally. He ruined me completely.

I can't even bear to say the words out loud. While in the hospital, Stoney, who's a member of the Devil's Riot MC, well, he's more than a member, he's actually the National President of the club, walked in on me as I was about to slice my wrist open. As much as I want to hate him for stopping me, I'm thankful to him. He's givin' me the chance to heal without being around those who are involved. If I want to be honest with myself, I couldn't stay there and see everyone being happy, moving on with their lives.

I've always been able to hide my emotions under a mask but since that day, I can't. I cry at a moment's notice or become infuriated over the smallest thing.

Stoney has been really good to me since moving me here, along with the other guys. For the most part, they've all given me the space I've needed. Usually, I seclude myself, staying in the room they gave me. The only person here who doesn't is Momma B. If I didn't feel so damn numb inside, I'd run the other way in fear most days. She has a way of scaring the shit out of someone with just a look. The club girls know not to fuck with her. Me on the other hand, I'm constantly getting the evil eye from a few of them. I don't know what their problem with me is since I'm not here to step on anyone's parade. I just want to be left alone.

Alone— that's all I want, to be by myself. I need time to deal, learn how to live with the knowledge that I'm no longer the woman I used to be. I'm no longer the woman who'd speak her mind no matter what. I'm no longer able to laugh at the simple things. I'm broken. No, actually, I'm not just broken, I'm completely shattered. My life is no longer mine. Even from the grave, Jake has taken control over me, just like he wanted.

Do I want to be the person I've become? No, I don't. I want to be me again, but that will never happen. My life has completely changed. Things that I always wanted; I'll never have. I will never be able to hold my own child in my arms due to the damage Jake did to my body. My heart breaks at that thought alone. Then there's Rage. When I needed him the most, he walked away. I really thought he was the one for me. He and I seemed to connect on another level, however, when it came down to it all, he left me alone to deal with everything on my own. I get the fact I couldn't stand anyone's touch, turning into a screaming lunatic when Rage and the club came after Lynsdey and me. I mean, I wouldn't have wanted to be around me either, but I still needed his presence surrounding me.

Leaning back against my bed, I close my eyes, envisioning what could've been. Thinking of the child I lost in the whole ordeal and the irreparable damage caused. I choked back a sob as someone knocks on the door.

"Come in," I call out to who I'm sure is Momma B. When the door swings open, I'm surprised to see it's not Momma B, but Stoney. "Um, hi, Stoney, what's up?"

"I hadn't seen you come out of this room recently, figured I'd come to check on you myself, sweetheart. What are you doing to yourself?" Stoney says, moving into the room, leaving the door open. He always does which I'm grateful for. I'm not able to be in a room by myself with a man right now. Anytime it happens, I freeze up, my breathing becomes harsh and sweat forms along my skin.

"I'm not doing anything, Stoney," I reply as my eyes follow him.

"That's what I'm talking about, Cleo. Sweetheart, it's time to start working through that head of yours. You're so fucking deep in your head. Do you know nights you finally manage to pass out, your screams wake every brother in this clubhouse?" The way Stoney crosses his arms over his chest along with the look I'm getting tells me I'm in for a lecture, not from the man who has been my friend but from the club president.

"I'm sorry, I didn't know I'd been doing that. I can find somewhere else to stay if me being here any longer is an inconvenience for the brothers. I . . ."

"You're not an inconvenience, sunshine. You just need to realize it's time for you to seek help. Someone to talk to. I don't give a fuck if it's me that needs to play psychologist as long as you get help," he says, interrupting me before I go any further.

"But I . . ."

Stoney raises his hand, stopping me from saying anything else. "Cleo, I love you like a daughter, and I'll help you any way

I can. When I walked into your hospital room to find you about to slit your wrist, I knew you needed help. I've given you plenty of time. Honestly, I've given you more than enough time to dwell in pity. It's time to start picking yourself up again. You realize when the brothers came up with Twister to get Izzy, you refused to come out of this room for days. They respected the fact you were not ready to see anyone but with that, you hurt Kenny and Lynsdey."

"I'm not ready to see any of them, Stoney. The idea of seeing them all happy hurts. I can't have what they have," I whisper, lowering my head in shame. I can't be around them anymore without feeling a sense of longing for the lives they all have.

"Cleo, sunshine, listen to me. None of them would ever judge you for the shit that's happened. You're a part of this family whether you want to be or not. I realize you're not ready to go back yet and I'm not gonna make you, although I have a feeling I'm not going to be able to stop you once Rage gets here," Stoney says, moving toward the door.

"What do you mean by that?" I say, snapping my head in his direction.

"Means your man is about to reclaim what's his. That's what it means." With that, he walks out of the room, leaving me flabbergasted at his parting words.

What the hell? Rage walked away from me. There is no way he'd be coming here for me. I mean, who would want someone as damaged as I am? I can't even give him the family he'd eventually want.

# CHAPTER **TWO**

## RAGE

Getting to the national charter took what felt like for fuckin' ever with traffic. Several accidents left us at a standstill or crawling for half the trip, along with having to stop to fill up leaving my ass numb. Finally pulling into the lot in front of the clubhouse, I climb off my bike, stretching my legs. The trip up here never takes as long as it has today.

"Damn, I don't think I can feel my ass," Burner grumbles, getting off his own bike.

"Shut up, fucker, we're here and I need a fuckin' beer. Then one of the clubwhores to suck my dick," Hades says.

"I could go for a beer myself," I say, moving for the door. I thought I'd know what all I'd say to Cleo before I got here, but I fuckin' don't.

Stepping into the main room of the clubhouse, I let my eyes adjust to the dim lighting. Several brothers approach as I make my way toward the bar. Damn it feels good to be back here. I grew up in this club with my dad being the Road Captain.

At the sound of a loud squeal, every one of my brothers shuts up and looks over to see my mom. "My baby boy, move out of my way, you bunch of assholes, and let me get to him." My mom is overly loud as she moves to me. I love my mom even though she seems to be a little nutty at times. She handles this life by the balls, though, no one fucks with her family. If they do, all hell will rain down on them.

"Hey Mom, how's she doing?" I say, hugging her to me. Damn, I've missed this woman. Doesn't matter she calls me every fuckin' day. There's nothing like being home.

"Travis, I swear to fuck, I love you boy, but I will not allow you to continue to cause any more hurt to that beautiful woman," my mom says sternly at my question, giving me a look of frustration.

"Mom, don't start on me about this right now," I sigh, grabbing the beer the prospect placed on the bar next to me.

"Well, what should I start with, huh?" she throws back, placing her hands on her hips.

"Momma B, let the boy enjoy his beer in peace. He just got here, plus, he's gonna need it," my dad, Bear, says, pulling my mom into his arms. I don't know what any of us would do without him when it comes to dealing with her. Everyone here either respects her or fears her.

"What do you mean I'm gonna need it? What's goin' on?" I asked, starting to become frustrated.

"Finish your beer and wait for Stoney, then we'll talk."

I just nod, downing the rest of my beer. It can't be that bad, can it? With everything that has happened in the past year, anything is possible. What could be going on now? Only one thing comes to my mind, Cleo.

As I opened my mouth to speak, Stoney walks into the room with a grim look on his face. Damn it must be bad. His eyes meet mine giving me a nod in acknowledgment as he moves in my direction.

"Rage, it's good to see you. Let's go in my office to talk," Stoney says, walking past me.

I nod in agreement, moving to follow him.

"You want us with you, brother?" Hades asked.

"Naw, man, go get your dick sucked or something," I say, slapping him on the shoulder.

"Alright, we're here when you need us."

Following behind Stoney, we walk into his office. "Have a seat," he says, moving behind his desk. I'd figured my mom and dad would have come in here as well but they stayed behind.

"What's going on?" I ask.

Blowing out a breath, Stoney pulls out a bottle of Gentleman Jack from one of the drawers in his desk, placing it in front of me. Guess whatever he has to say is gonna require more than just the one beer I've had.

"Rage, I've got some shit I gotta tell you and you ain't gonna like it. That being said, I'm glad you got your head out of your ass. Cleo needs you." Stoney lets out a sigh.

"What ain't I gonna like?" I grab the bottle, taking a healthy amount into my mouth.

"Cleo isn't doing well. Since being here, she's constantly in her head, never leaving her room unless one of us pretty much drags her. That being Momma B. We've all tried to get her to talk however, none of the brothers try to go near her unless it's involuntary. When one of the brothers comes near her, she begins to panic. She doesn't sleep much and when she does, her screams can be heard throughout the entire clubhouse." Stoney stops speaking to reach for the bottle, taking a swig, then another before continuing. "Before you got here, I'd just come from talking to her. I told her it was time to get help. Rage, she's so fuckin' deep in that head of hers, I don't even know if you'll be able to reach her. You walking away when you did was her undoing to everything."

"Why haven't you told me about this sooner?" I ask, clenching my fist, the need to punch something consuming me. They should have fuckin' told me. It shouldn't have gotten this bad for her. I'd have come to help her if I'd known.

"Truthfully?" he asks and I nod my head in answer. "I didn't tell you 'cause you needed to figure out what the fuck you wanted on your own. You didn't need someone to guilt you by telling you shit that was going on around here with her. She didn't need that and neither did you. You're here now, so what ya gonna do?"

"You still should have fuckin' told me. Doesn't fuckin' matter if you thought it would have guilted me into coming or not. Cleo is my fuckin' woman, always has been. I know I fucked up at the hospital that day, but I've always loved her. What I'm about to do, I need you, my mom, and all the brothers to stay out of my way. I'm claiming my woman and taken her ass home," I say, standing up and moving for the door.

"You got it," he says, grinning as he follows me back out into the main room.

Looking around, I spot Hades sitting at one of the tables with one of the clubwhores sucking him off while talking to Burner and Coyote. I shake my head, walking over to them. "Hurry up, brother, we're leaving soon as I come back down here."

"What the fuck? We spent all fuckin' day ridin'," Burner says.

"Just be fuckin' ready. I'm not waiting." I turn back to Stoney. "You might want to warn the brothers while I'm gone," I say and then move toward the hall where all the bedrooms are. From what I've been told, Cleo's been staying in my old room. I'm pissed at everyone right now for not telling me what's been going on around here— and myself included for not coming sooner.

I open the door without knocking, and Cleo screams at the unexpected intrusion. At first glance, I know she hasn't been takin' care of herself as needed. Her hair isn't shiny like it's supposed to be, and her purple color has grown out, showing several inches of dark blonde. She's also lost a good amount of weight.

"Lave, what are you doing to yourself?" I ask, using the short version of the nickname I'd given her the first night we met. She's Cleo to everyone else but to me, she's my Lavender. Ever since I met her, Cleo has always had light purple hair. I don't know colors but it's what I'd assume it to be.

"R . . . R . . . Rage, what are you doing here?" she whispers, her eyes wide as she takes in the fact I'm standing in her room.

"I'm takin' your ass home where you belong, that's what I'm doing here," I tell her as I stalk toward her. I don't give her a chance to say or do anything before taking ahold of her and tossing her over my shoulder.

Cleo kicks and screams as I carry her out of the room and out to my bike.

It's time for her to come home.

# CHAPTER **THREE**

## CLEO

I couldn't believe when my door slammed open with Rage standing there. I thought I was hallucinating but nope, there he was. I didn't know what to feel when he put me over his shoulder and carted me out of the clubhouse to his bike. I didn't go willingly either. I screamed, kicked, and used my fist to assault his ass. Didn't help that throughout the entire scene, no one stepped forward to stop him— not even Momma B.

Now, I'm sitting on the back of his bike, holding on tight, fuming at the way he treated me. I'm also confused with why I'm not freaking out at being so close to him. Usually, I panic when one of the guys from the club comes near me, but not Rage.

Riding behind him feels right like it always has. Even though I'm pissed, I feel safe with him. I'm thankful he doesn't have the Bluetooth turned on in the helmets as we ride. I'm not ready to talk to him yet. Not only due to the way he carted me out of the clubhouse like a sack of potatoes but because of everything else. He left me when I need him the most, and I'm mad at everything he doesn't know happened.

As we make our way back to my hometown, the same town everything happened in, panic begins to set in. Shaking my head, I try to clear my head of the memories attempting to assault me. Rage reaches down to squeeze my thigh reassuringly as if he can sense my unease. Maybe he does. From the moment we met, Rage has always seemed to be able to sense when something isn't right with me. For instance, when I would be working at Outlaw Racks and he'd be there with skanks flirting with him, it bothered me he didn't push them away like I figured he would have— no, the jerk simply ignored their attempts of rubbing up on him. Those nights, I'd make sure to stay away from their table. I didn't need to be getting into trouble.

When we get to town, I expect Rage to turn toward the clubhouse. It's not like I have a place there anymore. Even if I did, I wouldn't want to go there again. Too many memories involved with that place. Yeah, most are good memories and should trump the bad ones, but all the same, they're all painful.

My thoughts consume me as I hold onto Rage, trying to fight them off so I can see where he's taking me. When he turns into the driveway of the most gorgeous house I've ever seen, a gasp escapes me. The house looks just like the one I've always wanted— at least from what I can see through the dark. The porch light is on showing a beautiful wrap around porch with a swing in the corner. Growing up, I always loved going to my grandma's house and sitting on hers. I'd sit there for hours listening to the wind blow through the trees. The house itself looks to be a remodeled farmhouse.

"Come on, Lave, let's get you inside. I'm beat," Rage says, turning the bike off.

"Whose house is this?" I ask, climbing off from behind him.

"It's ours, Lavender. I just finished moving all your shit in here before coming to get you," he replies with a shrug.

Words escape me at his answer. Holy Mother of God, seriously? Why the hell would he do this? I thought he didn't want me after the last time I saw him.

"Babe, come on, I'll show you inside," Rage says, grabbing my hand and pulling me along the pathway to the house. My mind doesn't seem to want to get past his words as they keep replaying in my head.

Once inside, Rage lets go of my hand, placing it at the small of my back and guiding me through each room on the bottom floor of the house.

"I left the old furniture behind figuring we could go shopping for a new couch and shit like that. Tomorrow, we can go look as well as get groceries. I had brand-new appliances put in, I know how much you love to cook and bake shit. We'll have to get you pots and pans for it, the ones you used to have looked worn out. Upstairs, we have three bedrooms as well as a guest bedroom down here. I'll be staying in that one until you're comfortable with me being in your bed but that's a discussion for another day," Rage says.

"I don't know what to say, Rage," I whisper, looking up at him for the first time, noticing the dark circles under his eyes—he looks exhausted. He also hasn't shaved in days from the scruff on his face.

"There's nothing to say, Lave," he says stepping toward me. Rage reaches up and I flinch as he brushes a strand of hair behind my ear. "I'm gonna take a shower and hit the bed. If you need anything, don't be scared to come to me. I'm always here for you."

I don't move until I hear his door shut. What the hell is going on? Did I get sucked into some other dimension? After everything that happened, him walking away from me and now he wants us to live together. Fuck me, I don't know what to think about any of it.

Walking through the rest of the house, I head toward the stairs; I need a shower myself. Going to each door, I open them glancing in each until I get to the master bedroom— holy shit, the bedroom itself is huge, I mean *huge*. You could fit the other two rooms in here. The bed alone— I'm speechless. The frame looks to be hand carved. Running my hands along the smoothness, I wonder whose work this is. There's no way Rage did this. Even if he dabbles in woodwork, his stuff is usually a lot smaller than this. This bed had to have taken a hell of a lot of time.

Moving from the bed, I finish looking around the room. All my old clothes are hanging in the walk-in closet with boxes of my things labeled with what's inside. I shudder at the thought of some person I don't know touching my things. Continuing, I step into the bathroom. I could live in here. The shower is a walk-in with an overhead shower fixture, but that's not what I love most. It's the tub, it's huge just like everything else in the house. You could easily fit the two of us, leaving plenty of room to move around.

Seeing a basket on the side of it, I spot several bath bombs, I can't help the smile that forms on my face. He remembers my love of baths. I fill the tub, picking one of the bombs up and smelling it, it's lavender. Dropping it into the water, instantly it begins to fizz. I strip out of my clothes while the tub continues to fill up. Turning off the water, I step in and sink down into the water letting the lavender smell relax me as I soak.

Closing my eyes, I think about everything that's happened today. From the conversation Stoney and I had this morning to Rage coming in my room, carrying me out of the clubhouse and bringing me here. I'm confused as to why he would do all this after walking away. Is it out of guilt or does he really want me? I highly doubt if he knew everything, he would want me. I can't give him what another woman can— a baby. My body is too damaged.

Shaking my head, I finish up my bath before getting out to dry off. I don't even bother putting any clothes on when I walk into the bedroom, I simply crawl into the giant bed, my mind running a mile a minute. I don't want to fall asleep knowing what awaits me, my nightmares. It's the same every time.

Exhaustion doesn't let me fight, it never does. I fall asleep praying Rage doesn't hear my screams.

# CHAPTER **FOUR**

## RAGE

Fuckin' hell, it killed me to leave her standing there in the middle of the kitchen. I'd wanted to take her in my arms and let her know everything would work out. But I know better, she needs space to gather her thoughts. I only hope she doesn't get stuck in them.

Tomorrow is a new day and I intend to start pulling her out of it. She's gonna know I'm here with every intention of staying. Cleo is gonna know she's my ol' lady. I'll be makin' it known in the next church meeting too.

Jumping in the shower, my dick throbs for Cleo's touch. Wrapping my hand around my dick, stroking it as I close my eyes, I envision my hand as her mouth. The warmth of her mouth as she groans around my thickness. Grabbing her hair and fuckin' her mouth while she uses her hand to cup my balls.

A groan escapes me as I come— fuck, I miss having her body. This shit fuckin' sucks, jackin' off like a pubescent teenage boy, but I refuse to have anyone but her. Even in the time she was away, I refused the clubwhores' advances. They don't come close to the shine Cleo has.

Turning the shower off, I grab a towel as I step out. I'm exhausted after being on the road all fuckin' day along. Doesn't help I can't get my mind off what Stoney told me. I gotta figure out a way to help Cleo. Maybe get her into counseling. If that happens, I'll be sure she knows I'm sitting in on every damn one of her sessions. I refuse to let what fuckin' happened to Izzy happen again. Some bitches are just fuckin' crazy. The damn counselor tried to make Izzy feel inferior to being around her own family in an attempt to get her to leave Twister. What kinda person does that? And for what, to try and get a little dick? Fuck that. I'll be sure to be there to protect my woman from that sort of shit.

Grabbing my phone, I lay back in bed looking into the different forms of help I can find for her. There are different support groups and crisis centers specializing in working with traumatized victims.

I don't even realize I fall asleep. My dreams lately have been nothing but nightmares. They always rotate between my sister and Cleo. I wasn't there to help find my sister, but my head shows her looking the same way Cleo did— beaten, battered, and covered in blood. In my nightmares, I can never get to either of them. I watch as faceless men attack them; an invisible wall seems to keep me out of their reach.

I feel like a failure for not being able to stop them from being hurt. But this time is different, as I attempt to get to Cleo the wall breaks and for once, I hear her screams. Screams so loud they wake me. Bolting up in bed, I shake my head to clear it— only it wasn't the screams in my sleep that woke me but her really screaming.

Climbing out of bed, I rush up the stairs, needing to help her. Opening the door to what should be our room, it kills me to see her thrashing around in the bed as her screams grow louder, begging to whoever she's fighting in her nightmares to let her go. Quickly I climb in next her, pulling her against me, soothing her with my voice in her ear. Whispering sweet, gentle words meant to calm her. Finally, after what feels like hours rather than mere minutes, Cleo stops screaming and her breathing smooths back out.

Fuck, Stoney wasn't kidding about her screams in the middle of the night. Her nightmares must be worse than my own. I can imagine, especially after the bullshit she went through— add me walking away on top of it and Cleo's had enough to last her a lifetime. I swear I won't let anything else hurt her.

"Rest easy, Lave, I've got you. You're safe," I whisper, holding her in my arms. I drift off for the second time that night, only this time the nightmares don't come. That's when I realize she's not the only one who feels safe. With her in my arms, I'm just as safe. I may sound like a pussy, but I don't give a fuck.

---

I groan at the sun shining in through the windows, fuckin' hell we'll need to get some curtains or some shit. I can't stand the fuckin' sun being that fuckin' bright when I get out of bed. I'm not a morning person. I go to stretch, stopping myself when I remember Cleo being in my arms. Now, this I could get used to again. Damn if I didn't miss her sleeping in my arms at night.

Gently, I get out of the bed, not wanting to wake her up just yet. I don't know how she'd react to me being in bed with her, especially with me not wearing a damn thing. I make my way back downstairs to the guestroom and put on a pair of sweats. I go into the kitchen to start the coffee, it's the only thing we have right now. I can't live without my coffee. They call me Rage for a reason. I have a temper, but I can control it to an extent. I'm not one to fly off the handle. I save that shit for when I need a release, at which point, I find one of the brothers to spar with me. Not many of them will willingly go against me. Usually, it's Gadget, Dragon, or Hades who will take me on.

When the coffee is ready, I fix my cup. I hate all the sissy shit people put in their drinks. Leaning against the counter, I take in what all we need to get done today. I'm just finishing up my first cup when Cleo comes down the stairs.

"Morning, Lave," I say as soon as she enters the kitchen.

"Morning," she grumbles, moving to the coffee. She's not much of a morning person either, and she's never been one to drink coffee. According to her, it tastes like ass.

"When did you start drinking coffee?" I ask, lifting a brow as she takes a sip from her cup.

"I don't know." She shrugs her shoulders, leaning against the counter and cradling the cup with both hands.

"We need to get started, Lave. We got a lot of shit to get to make this house our home. You ready for that?" I ask her.

"No, I'm not ready, but I guess I don't have a choice in the matter. I'll go change and get ready," she says, stepping away from the counter, not looking at me. Cleo has barely looked at me more than a few times since I carried her out of Stoney's clubhouse.

"Lave, baby, you always got a choice in anything we do, but when it comes to you and me we're gonna work that shit out. You've always been my woman, even when I was too fucked in the head to stay at a time you needed me the most. I fucked up and intend to make it right between us. I love you, my Lavender. I hope you know that," I say, without intending to, but she needs to know just how I feel about her. I don't want her to be running the other way scared or wondering when I'll up and leave again.

"Rage, you don't want me, not anymore. I mean, seriously, you know what happened that day, but you don't know everything he did to me and planned to still do to me. By the time he was done, Lynsdey would have been dead while I was still alive as his pet. So please stop thinking we can be more than friends. I can't give you anything I haven't. I love you too, so much it hurts saying this to you, but you need to know we can't be together," Cleo says, ending on a sob. I stand there speechless as she makes her way back out of the kitchen.

I run my hands through my hair in frustration. Here I thought I could bring her home and fix the problems for her. Get her the help she needs and everything would go back to normal. We could start a family, be a family together. Fuckin' Jake fucked everything up. Punching the wall, my fist goes through the drywall and I don't even feel the pain of it.

What do I do now? Cleo is my fuckin' everything. I'm clueless right now as to where we should go. Fury begins to consume me at not being able to bring back the dead to send him there again. Shaking my head, I go get dressed, throwing on a pair of jeans and a tee, sliding my cut on before stepping into my boots.

If not for all the shit we need to get for the house, I'd be out of here now. I need to clear my head to figure out my next step.

Then it dawns on me, what I did when I started to heal after my sister's death. I run my fingers along the right side of my chest where I had my first work of art done. Maybe just maybe, I can start there. They say the right tattoo artist can work wonders in helping you start living again, it worked with me. Hell, it even worked with Thorn when he attempted to eat a bullet while we were still in the service. Thorn might just be the answer to get Cleo to talk to someone.

I only hope my next step doesn't fuck me over.

# CHAPTER **FIVE**

## CLEO

My heart aches as his words repeat in my head. He loves me. How can he love someone so fucked up on the inside? He hasn't even seen the scars marring my body. No one other than the doctors who first treated me have. I can't even look in the mirror.

Instead of taking the bike, he opts for a truck I didn't even know he bought. The ride is silent as we drive down the road. When we pull up in front of a building with the words *Devil's Ink*, I finally look over at him as he puts the truck in park.

"I thought you said we needed to get stuff for the house. Why are we here?" I ask confused as to why we're at a tattoo parlor. I didn't even know Franklin had one.

"We'll get to all that in a little while, first we're gonna do something else," he says, getting out of the truck without another word. I watch as he walks around the truck, coming to my door and opening it for me since I have yet to move. "Come on, Lave, you can't sit here all day. Move that sexy ass of yours."

My front brushes his as I slide out of my seat, unable to avoid touching him with the way he's standing so close.

Grabbing my hand, Rage walks to the door, holding it open for me to walk through first, never once letting go of my hand. Looking around, I see the emblem for the club hanging above the reception desk. This must be the clubs.

"Well damn, aren't you a sight for sore eyes. I mean shit, I saw you last night, well more or less, I saw you being carted out on this ass's shoulder," Burner says when he comes around the corner.

"Hi, Burner," I say quietly, not looking directly at him.

"What brings you two in here?"

"Want some work done, free-handed," Rage says, moving further into the room.

"Tell me more. I'm down for doing freehand anytime, brother. Whatcha want?" Burner gives Rage a huge smile.

"Not for me, for her," Rage says, pointing in my direction.

"Me!" I squeak out.

"Yeah, Lave, give it a try. I promise I'll be right here with you the entire time," he says quietly. Lifting my chin so my eyes make contact with his own, I realize he's serious about me getting a tattoo. Finally, I nod. I can do this without panicking—at least, I hope so.

"Alright then, you're in luck. I don't have any appointments until later today and if I need to, I can postpone them or hand them off to Badger," Burner says, leading the way toward the back. "This room is usually meant for certain types of tats, but I figure you'll be more comfortable here than anywhere else. Go ahead and figure out where you want this done while I get my shit. I'll be right back."

"Lave, babe, why don't you get a little shoulder piece or something. Just something small to start out with. If you want something else, you can always get more later," Rage whispers.

My shoulder would mean him seeing my back. Does he remember the marks? I'd been covered in so much blood that night, I didn't think the guys knew about the scars all over my body. Getting a tattoo means I can cover them, then I don't have to fear what others think of me.

Nodding my head, I look in his eyes. "Can I get something going across my entire back, from my shoulders to right at my pants line?" I ask.

"Whatever you want, Lave, it's up to you. Burner's good and I'll be right here the entire time. Why don't you go ahead remove your shirt and get on the table before he comes back in? I'd hate to kill him for seeing more of your beautiful body then he already is," Rage says then turns to give me privacy like that's going to make a difference in what he's about to see. At least when he sees it, I won't have to see his face.

Taking my shirt and bra off, I get on the table and wait for Burner to come back. It doesn't take long before I hear him come back in pushing a cart with supplies on it.

"Are we ready?" Burner asks, placing the cart next to me.

"Yes," I whispered, trying to stop the panic from setting in. These two men, one being the man I love more than anything, are about to see one of the many things I hide.

"Alright, then what are we getting? I see it's gonna be your back. Where and what would you like, Cleo?" Burner asks. I know he can see the scars, but he doesn't hint to them bothering him. Rage hasn't said anything or moved from where he is other than turning to face me.

"Lavender, tell him what you want." Yep, he can see them. I can hear it in his voice the way it becomes harsh. If not for the fact that I don't want either of them to see the worst of the scars along the front of my body, I'd be off this table in a heartbeat putting my shirt back on.

"I'm not sure what I want other than to completely cover my back. If you wouldn't mind, do what you feel would be best," I barely get it in a whisper as tears begin to fill my eyes.

"You got it, Cleo. Try and relax. I'm going to get ready to start. I need to clean your back and run a razor along the surface to prep for the fun part." At my nod, Burner runs something wet along my entire back then brings the razor behind it. When he's ready, I hear the buzz of his tattoo gun turn on.

My first instinct is to tense when he brings the needle down along my skin, but Rage must sense it. He grabs a chair and brings it to the front of the table where he begins to run his hand through my hair, soothingly. At his touch, I relax again back into the table. I don't know how long I lay there, Burner asked me several times throughout the process if I needed a break. I didn't.

Once I got over the initial pain of the needle going in and out of my skin, I started to enjoy it. It's almost as if Burner is helping me become someone new. I can say goodbye to the me who is scarred, and hello to the new me with ink. I've never thought about getting ink before now. And I'm grateful to Rage for thinking about this. Like always, he seems to know just what I need.

I may sound like a weak bitch right now and it's the truth, I am weak. As much as I'd love nothing more than to be my old self, it will never happen. Since the night Jake took me, my life has been nothing but a living hell. I've been scared out of my mind, of my own shadow. Not just that I jump at the smallest sound, but fearing what comes next.

I still stand by what I said earlier about him and I not being able to be together. I can't do it, physically or emotionally. Our dreams of being a real couple, a family, died the day everything happened.

Time seems to go by as I continue to listen to the buzzing of the tattoo gun. When the gun finally shuts off, I don't know what to think as I wait for Burner to clean my back.

"You ready to see the masterpiece I've created? Now, I'm not completely finished with it. We'll have to do another session in about three weeks to add the shading and color," Burner asks.

"Yes," I whisper, unsure how I'll manage it with him in the room. I'm not about to let him see the front. One— I don't need either one of them to see my scars that are in the front. Two—no way in hell is Burner seeing my boobs. I've always been self-conscious about them. Being a DD-cup, I'm used to all the jokes. I've heard them all. Hell, I've even been called the next Anna Nicole. It's one of the reasons I dye my hair purple. I might not be able to change them, however, I can change other things about myself.

Shaking my head to clear my thoughts, I realize both men have left the room. Guess they understood without me saying anything that I needed them out of the room. Standing up, I move over to the mirror, gasping at the work of art now covering my back. Tears well in my eyes. Burner really knew just what I needed. On my back is an outline of a beautiful woman surrounded by a bear, doe, snake, and wolf.

A knock on the door draws my attention back to the room instead of the work of art now covering my back.

"Lave, you ready for us to come back in? Burner needs to bandage your tattoo up so we can head out," Rage calls out through the door. Oh shit, I quickly grab my shirt, covering my front before letting him know they can come back in.

When the door opens, I can't help but look at the two men walk back into the room. "Why?" I simply ask into the room, tears falling from my eyes. Burner looks at Rage then back to me.

"My head told me it was what you needed," Burner says, shrugging his shoulders.

"What does that mean?"

"Cleo, I might not know everything you've been through but I know enough. Soon as Rage asked for freehand, my head drew up the image that now covers your back. I won't go into detail on how that works but I can at least tell you why I chose those animals for you. That is if you want me to," Burner says, going about bandaging my back.

"Please."

"They all stand for several things. The bear— strength,

courage, healing, and strong ground force. The deer— gentleness, innocence, vigilance, sensitivity, and the ability to regenerate. The snake— that can mean several things. But in this case, he stands for healing, primal energy, and transformation. Finally, the powerful wolf— instinctive, intelligence, and lack of trust. These animals are to represent your spiritual rebirth. As of now, they're your protectors. The four surround you to keep you safe, hide your scars, and let you start living again," Burner says, moving toward the room to clean up the equipment.

I don't know what to think let alone say to him, so I simply nod.

"Thanks, brother, means a lot," Rage says, moving to stand in front of me.

"No problem, brother. I've got you," Burner replies, stepping out of the room, pulling the cart with him.

"Come on, Lave, let's get your shirt on. We got shit to get done now," Rage says once the door closes behind Burner.

Rage helps me gently get the shirt on without messing up the bandage. Sucks I had to go without my bra, but there's no way I'd be able to wear it and not mess up my new tattoo.

"How about we go grab some food and decide what to do next?" Rage says, guiding me from the back of the tattoo parlor to the front entrance. I stop dead when I see several of the club members standing there. "Come on, Lavender, they're not gonna do anything. They wanted to see you with their own eyes," Rage says, wrapping an arm around my shoulders. I flinch but only slightly. It's strange, even though I flinch, I'm not as scared of his touch.

Maybe Burner's right about my spirit animals protecting me. I honestly don't know much on the subject. I'll have to look into it more.

I let Rage guide me past all his brothers, out the door, and into the truck where he helps me climb into my seat. Before he closes the door, he grips my chin, making me look directly at him.

"I'm sorry, Lave, so damn sorry I didn't protect you. You might not think we belong together, but we do. I'm gonna help you get to that point," Rage murmurs, his voice full of regret. I open my mouth to say something, anything, but words escape me yet again. I end up merely giving him a nod, lifting my hand to his cheek, stroking the ruff whiskers. Rage closes his eyes for a brief moment before pulling away and closing the door to go to his side.

Maybe, just maybe, I can heal from this.

# CHAPTER
# SIX

## RAGE

The feel of her hand against my cheek almost makes me come undone. It's the first time Cleo's touched me willingly. I get she's been home less than a day, but I've been dying on the inside without her touch for months. Having her touch me like she did set a fire in my soul I don't ever want to lose.

Earlier, when Burner was covering the scars on her back, red filled my vision. I knew about her having some scars, but when she first laid on the table, I saw what she wanted to hide. Kills me to know I never once asked her about the older ones. But then again, after Lynsdey went missing, I knew she'd never tell; probably think I wouldn't want her anymore. What she doesn't get, though, is with the scars or not, she's the most beautiful woman in my eyes.

I could barely keep myself from touching her earlier and now here I am in a fuckin' home goods store trying to be good about everything when I want nothing more than to strangle this woman. Cleo used to love going shopping, dragging me along with her whenever she could convince me to go, and usually it involved getting my mind blown with a blowjob. Otherwise, fuck that shit. I fuckin' hate shopping. I'd have preferred to get one of the ol' ladies who are Cleo's best friends to come do this. Unfortunately, I know she's not ready to face them just yet.

Shaking my head from my thoughts, I watch as Cleo finally picks up a set of dishes that weren't the cheapest set on the shelf. I had to put my foot down when we first got here about not picking out shit she really doesn't want. The house is ours, not just mine.

When Cleo has the cart loaded down and moves for the register, I finally speak up again. "You done, babe?"

"I think so. I didn't really look around the house to see what all you need, but for now this will do," Cleo says, looking up at me.

"Lavender, sweetheart, the house isn't only for me, it's for the both of us. I've told you already and I'll continue to tell you until you get it. You and me, we're happenin'. You might not agree with me yet, but you, Cleo, are my ol' lady," I murmur loud enough for her ears alone.

"Rage, you don't want me as an ol' lady. I promise you that if you knew everything I've been through, you'd run the other way," Cleo murmurs back, tears shimmering in her eyes. Guts me seeing the pain she carries with her.

"Lave, I ain't going anywhere, no matter what you tell me. How 'bout instead of going to finish this shopping trip, we grab some take-out and head home. I'll lay out some blankets on the floor and we can just talk. You and me, like we used to. Doesn't have to be any heavy shit, fuck, it can be about the sky being blue. I don't give a damn," I say, reaching up to brush a strand of hair fallen from her hair clip.

Cleo doesn't answer at first, simply stares me in the eyes searching for any deception I might be trying to pull on her. Finally, she nods her head in agreement. "Okay, that sounds nice. Can we do Chinese? I haven't had bourbon chicken and lo mein noodles in what feels like forever," she says.

"Yeah, Lave, we can get Chinese. That sounds good, actually, I might get the same thing." I can't help but hide my smile at the small win. To have Cleo at least willing to open up to me somewhat, I'll fuckin' take it. Might make me sound like a pussy but damn my woman needs to know she can open up around me. She needs to know I'm here for her and I'll do anything in my power to bring a smile to her face, to see her eyes light up at the sight of the smallest thing again.

Once I pay for everything, we head out. Quietly, we load everything in the back of the truck before heading over to the Chinese place Cleo introduced me to when I first met her. They've got the best noodles I've ever had. We've spent many nights eating from there.

I don't waste time after they have our food ready. When they say ten minutes, it's usually five and, boom, it's done.

On the drive back to the house, I glance over to Cleo several times, seeing her staring out the window while rubbing her hands nervously against her jeans.

"Lavender, babe," I say, gaining her attention. When she looks at me, I reach over, grabbing her hand. I feel her tense as I hold her hand in mine and I squeeze it. "You don't need to be nervous around me. I swear I'd never hurt you, Lave. I'd take a fuckin' bullet to the chest before ever laying a hand on you." The sound of Cleo's breath catching on a sob sends a knife into my gut.

We don't say another word throughout the rest of the ride. Both lost in our own thoughts. My mind keeps going back and forth between the past with all the shit my sister went through causing her to kill herself, moving forward to what Cleo's going through now. In my heart, I know they're two different scenarios, but my head keeps putting them together. Combining everything my sister dealt with to Cleo's. Only, it's not my sister's face but Cleo's.

As we pull into the driveway, I shake the negative thoughts

out of my head, needing to prepare myself for what Cleo may or may not say.

Whatever she says, I'll be here for her. She's more than my woman. Cleo's my life; hell, this woman is the air I fuckin' need to survive this world.

# CHAPTER
# SEVEN

## CLEO

My heart clinches at Rage's words. I don't know what to say right now, so I simply nod my head. Getting out of the truck, I follow him into the house. Again, taking everything in. I'm still having a hard time believing he bought this place for us. My stomach turns in knots at the knowledge of him and I being a family. There's nothing more in this world I want. I've always wanted Rage, ever since the first time I met him. The connection between the two of us had been almost instant. I still feel what we've always had but after everything, I doubt he will want me. Especially once I tell him. He deserves to know it all.

"Come on, babe, you start pulling food out while I grab a blanket," Rage says from behind me, guiding me into the living room. I take the Chinese food from him as he moves past me without saying a word. Kneeling down, I start pulling containers out. Doesn't take him long to go get a blanket.

Sitting down, we both eat silently at first. I can't stand the silence right now, not when I know he's waiting for me to be the first to speak. I lean forward to grab my drink and clear my throat, getting Rage's attention. I'm not stupid to think he wasn't watching me. Taking a sip of my drink, I place it back down on the floor. Sitting up straight, I place my hands in my lap, keeping my eyes on Rage the entire time.

Clearing my throat once more, I open my mouth to speak. "You said I didn't have to talk about anything serious, that it could even be about the weather. However, you need to hear this. You have to understand why we can't be together," I murmur, unshed tears forming in my eyes.

"Lavender, whatever you have to say won't have any effect on the way I feel about you. I told you I'm not goin' anywhere. I realize I fucked up when you were in the hospital by walking away, but at the time, I couldn't do it. Not when my head kept flashing back to things I was unable to stop from happenin'. I felt I'd let you down like I had my own flesh and blood." The anguish in his eyes as he speaks tells me how much he's been hurting.

"We'll see" is all I say before taking a breath to begin. "I'm going to start at the very beginning. Back when Lynsdey and I were in high school, she never wanted me to come to her house. We always met up somewhere else or she'd come to mine. Well, one day, I decided to go to her place and surprise her with a trip to the mall. When I'd gotten out of the car, screams could be heard from the woods. I knew it was Lynsdey's voice, and without thinking, I took off running, not knowing what was going on. When I found her, Jake was looming over her. I didn't know who he was at first, all I could see was my friend in trouble. So, I tackled him to the ground, trying to save my best friend. That was the day my life changed for the worse. Jake started stalking me. To this day, I'll never understand why he targeted me. I mean, I don't look like any of the other women who he raped. But he did. More than I care to admit.

"The first time Jake raped me, he told me if I ever spoke a word about what he was doing to me, he'd kill me." I pause, taking a breath before moving on. "Skipping forward to when he took me, I'd been heading to the hospital after what happened to Lynsdey. I'd been lost in thought, thinking about every possibility of losing my best friend that I didn't see the deer jump in front of my car. I swerved to miss it, hitting the ditch. Thankfully, the ditch wasn't deep, and I'd been able to get out. But by the time I did, a car came up next to me. Looking over to see who pulled up, it was Jake and Sofia. I didn't even get the car in drive before Jake was out of his and snatching me out of mine. He threw me in the back seat of the other car, ordering Sofia to take mine somewhere to hide it. Hell, I still don't even know where my car is. Not that it really matters, the thing was a piece of shit.

"But anyway, he drove in silence to the shack. The moment he put the car in park, that's when all hell broke loose. He raped me in the back seat of the car then dragged me by my hair inside, chaining me to a wall with my back facing him. Jake whipped me with something that had metal prongs. You can't imagine how much it hurt. After that, he left me there hanging for God knows how long. I could hear moans of pleasure from behind me. I do know that before he and Sofia left, he unchained me, moving me to another room where he placed a dog's collar around my neck, chaining me to the floor. Then he proceeded to rape me again while Sofia helped him. She pinched, bit, and scratched at my body as he slammed into me. The worst part of all that was when he ordered her to join him in fucking me." I can't stop the sob that comes out.

"Shhh, baby, you don't have to tell me anything else," Rage says, moving closer to me.

Shaking my head, I move back away from him. "No, I need to finish this. I don't ever want to have to repeat it," I tell him, trying to calm myself back down. Giving myself a minute to get my breathing back under control, I start again. "I don't know how long Jake and Sofia were gone, all I know is I woke up to choking on the collar around my neck. Jake forced me to walk on all fours to another room. I didn't even glance up until he said Lynsdey's name. He told her that she was the reason he did what he did to me. That I was to be used anytime he felt the need to punish her. I was to be his pet while she was to be his dark angel.

"He then proceeded to rape me in front of her. I blacked out from the pain of it. Then before you and the rest of the club got there, he'd forced me to give him a blow job," I say, keeping my eyes focused away from Rage. I take another much-needed breath. "I don't remember much after that until waking up in the hospital. I want to say that's a good thing but I'm not sure. The rest of this that I'm about to tell you, I want you to know I'm deeply sorry," I say, looking at him briefly. "I didn't know I was pregnant. The doctor told me it was early but confirmed we were gonna have a baby."

Tears stream down my face as I close my eyes. "I lost our child, Rage— before I even knew I carried him or her. I'm pathetic. I couldn't even protect myself let alone a child that you and I had created. And now, I can't even have any more due to the severity of the damage Jake did to my body. This is why we can't be together." I finally look Rage directly in the eyes. Tears are running down his cheeks. I quietly sit there and let him gather himself.

Keeping my eyes on Rage, I watch the different emotions cover his face. When he focuses on me, I don't know what to think when I'm instantly pulled into his arms. He's shaking as he cries into my neck.

"I'm so fuckin' sorry, Lavender. I swear if I could bring that motherfucker back from the dead, I'd do it only so I could do far worse than what he got. He got off easy for what he did to you, to us. I wish I'd know about the baby. Fuck, I would've never left you. You didn't need to go through that shit alone. And from now on, you're not. I might not be able to see you carry my child but, baby, we're a family. I'm never letting you fuckin' go," Rage murmurs all the while tears stream down his face.

I don't say another word, simply nodding my head as I

wrap my arms around him and cry. I cry for the loss of our child, and for myself. I didn't realize telling him would relieve so much burden off my chest. I only wish that what he says is true. He might wake up tomorrow and realize that the family he always wanted won't happen with me. Hell, there are plenty of women out there who would love nothing more than to sink their claws into him.

Day by day, I'll see if his words hold true.

# CHAPTER
# **EIGHT**

## RAGE

I've never been a crier, not even as a kid when I broke my arm in two places. Growing up in the club, I learned from my dad and all the other brothers, you never show weakness. I never showed weakness growing up, wanting to be tough like all the members of the club. I knew one day, I'd join them. Hell, even when it tore me apart on the inside, I didn't even cry the day I found out about my sister. But at the moment, tears fall down my cheeks as I take in everything Cleo has told me. I hate the fact she's gone through so much and on top of everything, lost a child. *Our child.*

Fury consumes me. It takes everything in me not to get up and storm out of this house. I want, no I need, something or someone to pound my fist into. But it will all have to wait. *Fuckin' hell!*

This wasn't supposed to happen. I hope the motherfucker is getting what he deserves in Tartarus. Or at least unable to escape 'The Phlegethon' that leads to Tartarus. See, our club's motto says, 'We Ride Through Hell To Get To The Other Side'.

And I fuckin' agree with this, however, I also believe in the Greek mythology legends of 'The Underworld'.

Hell, Hades and I have had more than one debate about it. Between the two of us, we can both recite all of Homer's and Virgil's books with as many times as we've read them. Some of the brothers like to fuck with us over the fact we read, but fuck them, keeps the mind going.

Taking a deep breath, I focus back on Cleo. I feel like complete shit for leaving her in the hospital that day. How fucked up do you have to be to leave when you're needed the most? I seriously fucked up big time here. How the hell she can even bear to be near me, I don't understand, but I'm not letting her go. We don't have to have a child in order to be a family. Yes, it would have been great to have seen her grow round, bringing life to this world but maybe there's something more out there for us. Even if that something is just the two of us.

"Cleo, I know I said it already, and I can say it a million times over, I'm so fuckin' sorry. I swear on my life, you won't ever go through something like this again. You and I, Lavender, we're gonna make this work," I whisper placing my forehead against hers. Cleo's breathing hitches as tears fall from her eyes. She really must have thought I wouldn't want her after everything she went through. Pulling her flush against my chest, I hold her, making sure I don't rub her back, knowing it has to be tender if not hurting.

My heart aches knowing just how much she needed me, and I let her down in more ways than one. And on top of everything, I let her leave thinking I was done. Even though that was never the case. I simply needed time to wrap my head around everything. My head was in a fucked up place the day we found Cleo and Lynsdey in that disgusting shack. Fuck, the place was straight out of one of those horror flicks Cleo would have me watch with her. Don't get me wrong, I got nothing against them but I much prefer an action movie with Bruce Willis or Steven Seagal.

"Rage, I know you think you need to say you're sorry, but you don't. It's me that needs to be the one apologizing to you," Cleo whispers after what feels like hours but had to be only minutes.

"Why do you need to be apologizing?"

"Because I wasn't strong enough to fight Jake and protect our child. I'm weak and you deserve someone stronger than me. Someone who can actually give you a child."

"Lave, do you not see what I'm seeing right now? When I look at you, I see this amazingly beautiful woman who's been through hell and back. The woman I see in front of me, she could have taken the easy way out of dealing with all the pain but instead chose the hard way. It might have taken a push from Stoney, but you did the right thing. I wish like hell it'd been me but I'm fuckin' glad Stoney stopped you."

"Actually, it wasn't only Stoney that stopped me, but you. Well, more or less, it was Stoney's words. He said if I took my life, I'd be taking you with me. Th . . . Tha . . . That you might as well be dead too. When he said those words, I knew I couldn't do that to not just you but your family, the club. I didn't want to be that selfish. So instead, I took his offer and left," Cleo says, sitting up as much as I'll let her. There's no way in hell I can let her out of my arms right now. *No fuckin' way.*

"I'm fuckin' glad his words stopped you and I hope time away from this place, from me, has helped because Lave, I'm not letting you out of my sight for a long ass time if ever," I state, givin' her a grin.

With a roll of her eyes, she sighs. "Well, I guess I need to call Kenny, see if I can get my job back."

"Like fuck you're gonna work at the bar," I growl out.

"I need a job, Rage, and Outlaw Racks pays really well," Cleo says, crossing her arms ready to fight me on this.

"Listen, Lavender, I'm not stopping you from getting a job, hell, you can come work at the garage with us. We need someone working in reception, but I don't want you at the bar anymore. I only just got you home and I'll be fuckin' damned if I want men looking at what's mine. You understand where I'm coming from."

"What's yours? Who says I'm yours? I know I didn't. As for the job at the garage, I'd love to work there," she says, throwing her attitude at me. Damn, I've missed it. It used to have a way of getting my dick hard and from the twitch it's givin' me right now, it still does.

"Oh, you're mine alright, you've always been mine. And you always will be," I tell her, leaning forward pressing my lips to hers gently not wanting to scare her away. She doesn't tense like she did earlier when I touched her but she is hesitant when my lips touch hers. Pulling back, I give her a reassuring smile that it's okay.

"I'm sorry," she whispers looking away.

"Nothing to be sorry about. You didn't do anything wrong. I shouldn't have tried to kiss you so soon. Even if it was a gentle kiss," I tell her.

"It's not that I don't want you to kiss me, because I do. I'd love nothing more than to have you kiss me, make love to me. But I'm not ready."

I cup her chin and turn her face back toward me, needing her to look at me. "No rush, Lavender, I'm not going to push you on this. I'm happy with the fact you're not tensing when I touch you right now. It takes time and I've got all the time in the world when it comes to you. When you're ready, all you gotta do is let me know," I tell her, and I mean every word of it.

Keeping my eyes on hers, I wait for her answer. Finally, Cleo nods her head. "Okay," she murmurs. She then proceeded to surprise me by leaning into me, hugging me. "I've missed you holding me."

"Then I'll hold you all night long," I murmur against the top of her head, holding her as close as I can.

We sit there for the longest time, holding each other before deciding to finish our food. Least it's Chinese food and is always better when reheated. Conversation flows easily between us, talking about what type of furniture would look good in the house to things happening with the club. I don't tell her much since most is club business. And I sure as hell stayed away from the topics of both Kenny and Izzy being pregnant. As much as those girls are gonna be dying to see Cleo, I don't think she's ready to see them. Not even Lynsdey.

Noticing the time, I tell her to head on up and get ready for bed while I clean our mess from dinner. It's not much to throw away but I take it all straight out to the trash can. Once done and the house is locked up, I leave the blanket right where it is for the time being. Making sure all the lights are off other than in the kitchen, I go to the guest room, changing into a pair of sweats. I don't want to freak Cleo out when she sees me coming into the bedroom. I told her I wouldn't rush her, and I won't. I merely want to hold the nightmares at bay for her. If last nights were anything to go by, I'd rather be right next to her when they start to grab hold of her.

Opening the bedroom door, the first thing I notice upon entering is Cleo laying in the middle of the bed already asleep. Moving toward her, I take in how tiny she looks with her head resting on the pillow I used last night. The closer I get to Cleo, I take in the frame of the bed surrounding her— a frame I designed myself. I'd been working on it since moving here. The headboard I carved out every single detail before sanding and staining several times to get the coloring it has. Once the clear coat was done, it was time to bring Cleo home.

Wanting to hold Cleo in my arms, I quietly climb in, gently pulling her against my body. This is the feeling I've missed all these months without her. Kissing the top of her head, I relax more into the comfort of the mattress. Closing my eyes, I fall asleep instantly.

# CHAPTER
# NINE

## CLEO

Warmth consumes me as I slowly wake up. For the first time in I don't know how long, I slept without waking up to nightmares— for that matter, I didn't even have one. Weird. Stretching my body, I tense at the realization I'm not alone. Looking down, I see an arm draped across my stomach holding me to said body. I don't have to look over my shoulder to know who's arm it belongs to. Rage. He must have come in here after I'd fallen asleep. Looking over my shoulder, I see the very man who holds my heart in his hands. His expression right now is peaceful compared to when he's awake.

It's one of the things I was drawn to when I first met him. I remember watching him walk into Outlaw Racks like it were yesterday. Lynsdey and I were finally in a good place after everything Jake put us both through. Working for Kenny helped, she became a close friend almost instantly. Kenny never really acted like a boss and treated everyone like a friend even the bitches that came in acting like they wanted a job. The only time you saw her turn into a bitch was when you go to screw her over. That day the club came into Outlaw Racks though, I saw the men come in. At first, I'd been a little nervous considering my past but then I glance at him, and I knew I wanted him to touch me. Looking him over from head to toe, I could appreciate a man who knew how to wear a pair of jeans. But what really got me were his eyes. The haunted look he carried in them. His eyes spoke more than anything and when they connected with my own, I'd been a goner. Hell, I still am.

Turning my head back around, I move to get out of the bed without waking him up. The bathroom's calling for me. I definitely don't wanna breathe dragon breath in his face. Seriously, who wants that? I also need coffee. I've never been one for the stuff but recently, it's grown on me and I like to have at least one cup.

Finishing up in the bathroom, I quickly run a brush through my hair, placing it on top of my head in a messy bun. Throughout the entire process, I refuse to look in the mirror. I don't need to see what I look like; I already know. Before everything, I used to take a good thirty to forty-five minutes making sure I looked good. I guess you could say I'd been a little conceded. Now, though, I couldn't care less. My nails are short from my biting them. My hair is a hot mess in itself. I don't need a mirror to know my roots are a quarter way showing. I honestly don't give a damn anymore. Granted, I loved my purple hair, it's the reason Rage started calling me Lavender.

Shaking my head, I walk out of the bathroom, glancing over to the bed where Rage is still asleep. I'm sure he won't be for much longer, especially once he smells the coffee. Once the coffee pot is ready, I press the 'brew' button. While waiting, I take my first real look around the kitchen. I've been here for a little more than twenty-four hours and I haven't had a chance to take it in. I'm in awe of how beautiful it is. Then it hits me, this is *my* kitchen. I love to cook anything from Carolina style BBQ to Baked Spaghetti. All the appliances look like the ones you'd find on the show 'Chopped'. A smile pulls at my lips thinking about the many times I'd curl up in Rage's arms to watch them race to make the best dish. Never once did Rage complain about it.

The beeping from the coffee pot lets me know it's ready and draws me from my thoughts. Not knowing where the coffee cups are, I grab the one I used yesterday out of the sink. Nothing wrong with using a day-old cup long as you rinse it out good. I make my cup and head out on to the back porch to enjoy the fresh air since there are no chairs to sit on inside. I guess today we have to go look for the furniture we were supposed to have gotten yesterday.

Instead, he'd taken me to get the most amazing tattoo started. I can't wait to see the finishing product. It's the only thing I want to see in a mirror. I'm going to have to get Rage to put lotion on it this morning. You'd think it would be more tender considering the amount of work that Burner did but other than being a tad sore, it doesn't bother me in the least.

Sitting down on the steps, I hold my coffee cup with both hands taking in the view. It's beautiful. I don't know whether it has to do with telling Rage everything I did last night or if it's something else but for the first time since that night, I can breathe even if it's a little bit. I don't think I'll ever be able to get over losing our child. I like to imagine it was a little boy that had his daddy's magnificent green eyes. It hurts not being able to know if the baby was a boy or girl. It wouldn't have mattered either way. I wish more than anything that I could carry a child still, but the extent of damage done to my body left me unable to do so. Sucking in a breath, I try to keep the tears at bay. I told Rage all I'm willing to tell him about what happened. He doesn't need to know the severity of the rest. The parts that will haunt me for the rest of my life.

"Lave, babe, what are you doing out here?" I jump at Rage's voice. I didn't hear him come outside. Turning my head, I notice he's only wearing a pair of low riding sweats.

"I'm just enjoying the view while drinking my coffee."

"Your mug is empty, babe. Want me to refill it for you?" he says, holding his hand out for it.

"No, I can do it. Sit and drink your coffee, I'll be right back." I stand to get up.

"Okay." Is all he says as I move past him.

Inside, I pour myself another cup and head back out. If we're gonna do this, live together, maybe we can get some outdoor furniture as well. It'd be nice to have a swing or something to sit on instead of the steps.

Sitting back down next to him, we quietly sip our own coffees for a few minutes, taking in the peacefulness around us. Looking at the trees, the wind makes the tops of them dance back and forth.

"How does your back feel this morning?"

"It's nothing too bad, a little sore, nothing I can't handle. Besides who could be sore after sleeping in such an amazing bed. The headboard is gorgeous."

"I'm glad you like it so much since I carved the headboard myself. Want me to put some lotion on it before we head out?"

"If you don't mind, but what do you mean you carved it?" I ask shocked at him nonchalantly throwing in the fact he designed something so beautiful.

"When it comes to you, I'd do anything you needed me to do, and as for the headboard, yeah I wanted you to have something special no one else would have," He smirks drawing a small smile to my face.

"Then let's finish our drinks so we can get started. We have a lot to get done today. I'm still not sure about this but I want to give it a try. I really do. I'm just a little leery." I say quietly changing the subject. Right now I'm unable to focus on what he just told me. I just can't.

"Why's that?"

"Because it's too good to be true," I tell him honestly.

"Lavender, there's nothing, and I mean nothing, I want more than you in my life. You're it for me, always have been. From the first time I saw you across the bar, eye fuckin' me, you've been it," he says, turning his body to face me completely.

"I'm scared you'll regret being with me when I can't give you anything other than myself. And that I won't be enough for you. You're gonna want to have kids and I can't physically carry one. Not anymore." Tears fall down my cheeks.

"Babe, you will always be enough for me. No matter what. If we decide we want to have kids then we can talk about our options. You saying you can't physically carry one doesn't mean we can't get a surrogate or hell, we can adopt maybe even become foster parents. There are plenty who need a good home," Rage says gently, wiping the tears from my face.

This man is more than I could ever ask for.

"Okay," I whisper, taking a breath.

"Good, now let's go get ready. I'd like to be sitting on a fuckin' couch tonight," he says, standing up before holding his hand out to help me.

"Then let's get to it." I give him a smile.

---

"Are you fuckin' kidding me? Babe, seriously, just pick a damn set and be done with it. For fuck's sake, stop askin' me which one I like better. I couldn't care less what it looks like long as it's not flowery or pink. All it needs to be is comfortable for me to sit my ass on when I'm watching the Steelers whip the Patriots asses," Rage mutters becoming frustrated at the fact I can't make my mind up on getting the three-set with the recliner or getting a sectional that has the reclining couch.

"If you'd just pick between the two of these we would be done already." I put my hands on my hips annoyed at the fact he won't help me pick. I've already picked everything else out furniture wise for the house. I found a beautiful little four-seater kitchen table and a dining room table that seats twelve. I also picked out a coffee table with matching end tables. Shoot, I even found a lamp set that would look amazing in the living room. The bases of them are teal and black swirl. I loved them the second I spotted 'em. Now, if he'd just pick between the two sets, we'd be done already.

"It doesn't matter to me which one, it's whatever you want."

"Ugh . . . fine, let's go with the 3 piece set, it would look better in the living room anyway," I say turning to walk away.

"Works for me. Let's get this all finished up. We still got to go get you some more clothes and shit, then go to the grocery store."

"I don't need any more clothes. I have plenty at the house. You know, the ones you packed and put in the closet," I tell him sarcastically. I mean, I know I lost some weight but what I have will work.

"Lave, you need clothes that fit, not just some pants that require a tight belt to stay up. Since being in this damn store alone you've had to pull your damn pants up more than once. So, we're gonna go grab you some more shit, got me?"

I bit the inside of my cheek to keep myself from snapping at him. He's already spending enough money on all the furniture for the house we're getting today, he doesn't need to be buying me clothes when I don't need it. I can gain the weight back. Long as I eat, which I have no doubt he will be sure of.

"I asked you if you got me, babe?" Rage growls out grabbing me by my waist. He's been doing that more today, touching me. Not much but enough for me to notice.

"I got you Rage, I still don't see the need to go spend more money than we have to when you're about to drop a good amount in here."

"I don't give a damn about the money. I've got plenty of it saved up. Even after buying the house," he says, leaning down to press his forehead against mine. "Let me do this, Lavender. I want to take care of you and if it means getting you clothes that fit, then so fuckin' be it."

"Okay, Rage," I whisper, my stomach feeling like it's doing somersaults. When he says things like that, I can't help giving in. With everyone else, Rage is a hard man to be around but with me, he's always shown me a different side of himself.

"Good, now let's get this handled. I'm gonna get Ace and Shadow to come pick it up and take it to the house."

"Ace and Shadow, who are they?" I ask lifting my brows. I don't think I've ever met them.

"Prospects."

"Oh, ok."

"You've met Ace but not Shadow."

"I don't know who either of them are but I guess since I'm back, I'll meet them at some point."

"Yeah, Lave, you will. When you are ready to go to the club, I'll take you to see everyone. I know the Ol' Ladies are dying to see you," he says, giving my hand a squeeze.

"I don't think I'm ready to face them yet. They probably think I'm weak for everything, you know with what I tried to do and then leaving without a word to them."

Rage doesn't respond right away but gives me a weird look like I'm missing something then proceeds to pay for everything, informing them of who will be by to pick it up shortly.

When we get in the truck, Rage starts the engine, however, instead of putting it in reverse to head out, he turns to me. "Lavender, do you remember when Izzy was at Stoney's club?" I nod remembering something happened though I stayed in my room, refusing to come out, not wanting to be around anyone. After Twister and everyone from here left, I'd finally come out.

No one ever spoke a word about what has been going on when I was around though. I never asked either. "It's not my story to tell but you might want to talk to Izzy. Out of all the ol' ladies, she'd understand you more than anyone. She's been through hell and back. I'll tell you that much and I'll also tell you those women miss the fuck out of you. There's no way they could be pissed or think of you as weak for what you attempted to do. Fuck, babe, you're one of the strongest women I've ever met besides my mom and those women. Hell, you're probably stronger," he murmurs while pushing a loose strand of hair that has fallen from my messy bun out of my face.

Maybe I should reach out to the girls. I know Lynsdey's been through hell, same as Kenny. I don't know about Izzy since I wasn't here, and I should've been. I'm a shitty friend for not being here when she needed her friends. I should've gone to her when she'd been up at Stoney's club. Fuck a donkey, I'm a horrible person for cutting them out of my life like I did. All three of them would've been there for me like I'd have been for them.

I need to make things right with all three of them, let them back in. I hope they can forgive me.

# CHAPTER
# TEN

## CLEO

The rest of the afternoon seemed to fly by. Rage drove us to my favorite store and even with my protests, we left with several bags full of everything from new jeans, t-shirts, yoga pants, and more. I tried to put things back when he wasn't looking only to find him picking something else up. I even got some new panties and bras. I drew the line when he went to the cosmetic section. I don't need or want any of those things. At least not right now. I love my make-up, especially eyeliner and mascara. I'm just not ready to get back to wearing it. The mere thought of getting dolled up turns my stomach. Yes, dolled up. Girly, sexy, hot, call it any of those names, it's all the same. I used to love it but it drew a lot of attention my way, attention I don't care to ever draw again.

Now, we're at the grocery store, working our way through, aisle by aisle. We've already filled one cart. That's what happens when you have a completely empty kitchen.

"Lave, how much more shit do we need?"

"We've only been through half the store and still haven't gotten to the meats yet, Rage."

"Fuck, at this rate, you're gonna buy out the whole damn store."

"It's not my fault we need food in the house for me to cook, otherwise, we'd survive on coffee alone," I say picking up flour and sugar.

"Cleo," someone screams from down the other end of the aisle.

I jump, nearly dropping the items to the floor. Looking up, Kenny is speed walking toward us pushing her own cart. She has an infant carrier in the middle of it. My heart starts to pound. I'm not ready for this. The last time I saw her, she'd still been pregnant with her little boy, and now, I'm about to come face to face with the reality. Both her and Lynsdey have given birth to healthy babies— while I lost my own child in the same time period.

Sucking in a breath, I finally speak up. "Hey, Kenny."

"Hey? That's all you have for me, bitch?" Kenny says, putting her hands on her hips like she's pissed at me. I don't blame her for it either. I open my mouth to respond but she beats me to it. Pulling me into her arms, hugging me as she whispers, "God, I can't believe you're home. Finally, you wouldn't believe everything that has happened." When she pulls back, she smiles. "You're coming to the clubhouse tonight. We need to have girl time and catch up. Lynsdey and Izzy will be pissed to know I saw you before they did. We've missed you so much, Cleo, please come tonight."

Looking over to Rage for help, I don't want to hurt Kenny but I'm not ready to go there yet.

"I don't know about tonight, Kenny," Rage speaks up— thank God.

"Oh, for the love of llama spit, Rage, you've had her to yourself the last two days. Yeah, we knew you went to get her. Your momma even called all of us laughing about what you did. Carrying Cleo out of the clubhouse in a fireman hold. Seriously. Talk about dramatic much. Swear the lot of you are nothing more than cavemen. Do we need to invest in clubs for you to beat each other with next or would it just be easier to piss a circle around us? No, you're coming tonight, no ifs, ands, or buts about it. We want time with our girl. You hear me?" In Kenny fashion, she doesn't wait for a response from either of us. "Don't make me come find you guys." She throws that last line over her shoulder, steering her cart back down the aisle.

I don't know what to say as Rage and I stand there. Kenny is a force to be reckoned with when she wants to be and damn if I don't believe her about not coming to find us if we don't show up tonight.

"Guess we're going to the clubhouse tonight," I say looking up to Rage's face. The shit-eating grin he has right now says it all.

"Might as well get it over with. You know those girls will do exactly what she said. Should've known you couldn't keep them away forever, babe," Rage murmurs, placing a kiss to the top of my head. God, the more he touches me the more my body is reminded of his gentleness and it warms me all over. I shake my head— I don't need to be having any kind of thoughts about him warming my body. That will lead to wondering about other things I'm sure as hell not ready for.

Turning back around, I start moving again, ready to get this trip over with.

We spend the rest of the time joking and laughing as he takes my mind off what's to come later on. Finally making our way to the registers, we work together to unload everything from the carts. I cringe when the cashier tells us the total. Maybe I did go overboard a little. Groceries aren't cheap, that's for sure.

"Come on, babe, let's get this shit home and relax a little. We've got some time to kill before we head to the clubhouse. The prospects should be at the house unloading all the furniture too. So, you'll be able to tell them exactly where you want it.

Hell, they can even unload the damn groceries too," Rage says after paying.

Once everything is loaded into the back of the truck, we make it to the house in record time. Rage was right, the prospects are there unloading a moving truck with our new furniture inside. Getting out of the truck, I go to start grabbing groceries.

"Leave it, babe, let the prospects get them."

"I'm capable of helping, Rage."

"Babe, you gotta put the shit away. They can help me bring it to you in the kitchen."

"Fine," I huff going inside and waiting for them to bring everything in.

Doesn't take me long to get the groceries put away once they're all out of the bags an sorted on the counters, from items to go in the refrigerator and freezer to the cabinets. I'm a little OCD when it comes to them being placed right. Always have been. Comes with the territory of liking to know when I'm reaching for something, it's right where it should be.

"Lavender, come take a look to see if this is where you want it. Fuck, this furniture is heavier than it looks, I don't wanna have to move it around more than I have to," Rage calls out from the living room.

A smile breaks out on my face at the tone of his voice. Seriously, the man can probably bench press the couch without breaking a sweat. Stepping just inside the room, I take in where they placed the furniture. They've placed the couch in the center of the room with the recliner on one side and the loveseat diagonally. With the way they have it set, the room looks cozy and nowhere near closed off. They even placed the end tables where they should be with the lamps. I knew they would look good with this set. "Looks great, guys. You did a good job, thank you," I say.

"Good then these two can get out of here," Rage says more to Ace and Shadow than to me.

Neither says a word as they leave.

"You could have at least given them a beer or something before kicking them out. I mean, they did just help bring all the furniture in here and helped unload the groceries," I mutter placing my hands on my hips.

"Babe, they're prospects, it's their job to do whatever we fuckin' tell them. Besides, prospects aren't allowed to drink."

"Wait, what? Why?" I ask confused.

"Because, Cleo, when someone wants to prospect, they've got to be able to prove themselves to be worthy of being one of our brothers. And one of the rules for being a prospect is don't drink. They've got to be able to withstand being around booze without losing focus on what could happen. With all the shit our club's gone through, we want to make sure our prospects have our backs before we even decide to vote them in. If we can't trust them to stay sober when needed, what's to say they will be able to focus on other shit when asked."

I nod in understanding as I listen to Rage explain. As silly as it sounds, I get it. You've gotta be able to trust someone with the smallest thing.

A tense silence falls between us as we stare at each other from across the room. Now, with everything done for the day besides going to the club in a little while, I don't know what to do. Before everything, I'd be in his arms in a heartbeat, it was one of my favorite things to do.

"We need to put some more cream on your tattoo soon. Don't want it drying out. Why don't you go grab the stuff while I find us something to watch on tv until it's time to head to the club. We can pick something up in town for dinner."

"Were you not with us when we almost bought out the grocery store? I am not eating more takeout when I'd prefer to cook. How about I fix us up some dinner really quick, then you can put that stuff on my back," I suggest.

"Works for me. Gotta admit I miss your cookin', Lave," Rage says, moving to stand directly in front of me. "Fuck, Cleo, I've missed that smile." The smile he's speaking vanishes from my face as he touches me. Running his fingers along my arm. God the feel of him touching me sends bolts of lightning through my body. I want nothing more than to jump him. What would he think if he saw my stomach? He saw my back yesterday while I got my tattoo. I'm sure he thought it was bad but he hasn't seen anything until he sees my front. For that matter, I can't stand the sight of it.

"Umm, I'm gonna go start dinner now," I whisper, turning to go to the kitchen. I don't make it half a step when Rage stops me by bringing my back flush to his stomach. Panic hits me at the movement. Standing there, I can't breathe, my vision becomes a blur. The feeling of darkness swarming around me starts to seep in.

"Breathe, Lavender, remember, it's only me here. I'm not gonna hurt you. I'd never hurt you, babe, not in a million years," Rage whispers running his hands along my arms with the barest touch. "That's it, breath with me, Cleo, you're okay."

Once my breathing is under control, I sag against Rage's chest, soaking in his warmth.

"I'm sorry, babe, I didn't realize you'd react that way," he murmurs against the top of my head. I know he didn't mean it and I shouldn't have reacted the way knowing it was only the two of us here, but it was on instinct.

"It's okay," I whisper, turning to face him. "Other than your little touches throughout the day, I haven't allowed anyone close enough to touch me let alone have their body against mine."

"I get it, Lave, it's out of habit, wanting to have you in my arms."

"I know, how about you hang with me in the kitchen while I cook and we can talk more. Maybe even find a way out of going to the clubhouse later."

"Can't get out of going tonight. I got a text earlier. We have church tonight. It'll give you some time alone with the girls. If you wanna come home after church, we can, okay?" Damn, I wanted to keep from going to the clubhouse.

Nodding, I go about fixing our dinner while he watches me. All the while, wondering if he'd been with anyone else. I can't be pissed with him over it if he had but I don't want to run into any of his easy lays. Those clubwhores are nothing but a joke. Thinking that if they walk around in barely any clothes the men will fawn all over them. No self-respect for sure. These men deserve more than they offer. Hell, it takes a woman like Izzy, Lynsdey, and Kenny in order to handle this life.

I wish I could be more like them. Where those women show strength, I'm weak. As much as I want Rage, I don't know if I'm strong enough for this life. A life where he needs a woman that can be his strength, not bring him down.

# CHAPTER **ELEVEN**

## RAGE

If I could've gotten out of tonight's church, I would've. However, when your Prez calls an emergency church meeting, you get your ass there. Being Road Captain, I take my job seriously. If I don't, it could end up getting one of my brothers hurt.

I didn't want to leave Cleo in the main room even if all the ol' ladies were swarmed around her. Shit, those women pounced her the moment we walked through the door. I'd barely been able to tell her I'd be back soon when Kenny threw her attitude at me telling me Cleo would be fine and to leave them the hell alone to catch up. Knowing Kenny, I'd thrown my hands up as I backed away shooting a grin at my woman. 'Good luck,' I mouthed to her, gaining a beautiful smile from her in return.

Now, here I am, trying to keep my thoughts on the meeting.

"Alright brothers, got some information today I found somewhat disturbing. Took it to Gadget to look into and I didn't like any of the shit he was pulling up. We found out the Dragons

Fire MC is in bed with the Diaz Cartel in Cuba," Twister announces, looking directly at me.

"What the fuck?" I roar, the Diaz Cartel had been keeping quiet for years ever since I came back from overseas, slaughtering several of their top men trying to get to Miguel Diaz for what he'd done to my sister. The fucker slipped through my fingers and I hadn't been able to find him since.

"Calm down, Rage," Twister orders. "I get you're pissed, we all are. Everyone in this room besides Badger here knows what Miguel Diaz did. Fuck man, Horse and I were there, we saw the shit firsthand."

"Why didn't we know the Dragons Fire MC was working with Diaz?" Burner asks. Looking at him, I grimace. He'd been dating my sister at the time. Wherever you saw her, Burner was right behind. Before I'd left for overseas, Burner came to both dad and myself asking for permission to marry Janie. We'd given it to him, proud to call him family. I found out not long after leaving he'd asked her, and her response made me laugh.

In my mind, I can still hear her laughter when she told me about it. How he'd taken her for a ride and asked her on the side of the road after making her think they'd broken down. Then not even a month later, she was gone. Took the club weeks to get her back. Janie was unable to deal with it all and took her own life. Left everyone to deal with the pain. I used to be pissed thinking she was selfish for taking the easy way. But then it dawned on me why and I understood. Burner and I'd gone on a rampage after the funeral, taking out as many as we could but the sick fuck Miguel got away. We haven't heard anything from the Diaz Cartel for years, why come to the surface now?

"According to the information I've found, Dragons Fire MC only recently started working with them. Last I checked, they'd been dealing with the Alcazar Cartel. With them switching the way they have, the Alcazar Cartel isn't too happy with them. They were supposed to be transporting a shipment for them. Instead, they handed the shipment over to Diaz," Gadget says, keeping his eyes on the screen in front of him. A second later, he has the information on the big screen TV for us all to see. The fucker is a damn genius when it comes to technology.

"You all know what this means?"

"It means they've cast the first fuckin' stone, Prez," Burner growls out.

"Exactly, now, I'm not callin' lockdown or anything right now, but that doesn't mean we don't keep our eyes open. We have a shipment coming in two weeks, are we ready?"

"Yeah, Prez, the last one went according to plan. I think we should take the same route," Thorn suggests.

"I agree, the roads we took kept us off all main roads," I say nodding my head in agreement, trying to keep my head straight. Now that the Diaz Cartel has resurfaced, it's time to finish what Burner and I started. Looking across the table at Burner, he nods in agreement. Miguel Diaz will meet his end by our hands, whether the club is at our backs or not.

The rest of church is spent going over the list of artillery coming in, where it will be heading, along with when to set up for the next shipment. Since Grigory took over being our contact with the Russians, it has been moving smoother than in the past.

As church comes to an end, Twister turns attention back to me. "How's Cleo doing?"

"I'm not sure. Honestly, I guess you can say she's doing the best she can. Cleo's been through a lot of shit. Everyone here knows the state we found her in. Last night she opened up some, telling me about when Jake had her. I'm sure she didn't disclose everything," I say shaking my head. "What she experienced is far worse than any of us could imagine. Out of respect for my woman, I won't go into detail, however, I will say if that motherfucker were still alive, I take my time killing him slowly."

"I'm sorry, brother," Thorn speaks up placing his hand on my shoulder squeezing it.

"Same, brother, know the club's here for both of you," Twister says.

"Is there anything we can do for Cleo?" Horse asks.

"Actually, VP, there is something the club could do for her. Cleo wants to go back to work and I don't want her working at Outlaw Racks. Any way we can put her at the garage in the office?" I ask. Cleo might be pissed about not working at the bar, though I think she'll really enjoy being at the shop. I definitely would.

"Jobs hers, Cleo can start any time she wants," Horse responds without even having to think about it. All the brothers love her like a little sister. Hell, all the ol' ladies have a special place in all our hearts. Even before they became ol' ladies. Kenny was Horse's mystery woman years ago and they found each other again. Lynsdey had Thorn twisted around her finger within minutes of meeting her, if not for Burner being drunk and Horse attempting to stop him from doing something stupid, they wouldn't have gone through what they did. Then there's Izzy, everyone has a soft spot for her. She fooled everyone into thinking she was this easy, fun going person when inside, she'd been dying of grief. Blaming herself for the death of her brother. Fuck, she had it rough. Thankfully, Twister stopped her from doing something extremely stupid. Now they're expecting their first child.

Fuck, I can imagine Cleo right now out in the main room. How she must be feeling sitting with her friends who have either had a child or are expecting.

"Fuck," I mutter out without meaning to.

"What up, brother?" Twister asks lifting a brow.

"It's nothing. Hell, it's no.. . . . nothing, Prez. Shit, I just don't know how to say it." Everyone at the table grows eerily silent at my words.

"What do you mean?" Thorn asks sitting forward.

"Cleo lost our baby," I blurt out unable to stop the words from coming out.

Throughout the room several mutters of words are spoken in harsh whispers, a few of them don't say a word but the tension fills the room.

"I'm sorry, brother," Thorn is the first to speak up.

"Yeah, brother, you have the club's condolences," Twister says, tapping his fist against the table.

"Thanks, brothers, I only found out last night."

"Fuck man, you mean Cleo didn't tell you she was pregnant before all that shit went down," Burner speaks up for the first time.

"Naw man, she didn't even know she was carrying our child until the hospital told her. Now she . . ." I stop, sucking in a breath, "With the damage done to her body, Cleo can't carry a child even if we wanted to try again," I finish on a harsh whisper.

No one says a word as they realize what I did last night—the true pain of everything my beautiful woman has gone through. That's without me even telling them her story. That's not for me to share. Hell, the only reason I even said anything about the baby is so they'd be prepared to deal with their own women if and when they do find out.

"Alright brothers, enough with this emotional bullshit. Let's get out to the main room, enjoy a beer or two," Twister says, banging the gavel down on the table.

Yeah, a beer right now sounds pretty damn good. Getting up, I walk out of the room followed by all my brothers. Walking into the main room, I stop, not expecting what's in front of me.

Fuck, not this shit again.

# CHAPTER **TWELVE**

## CLEO

Emotions are a crazy thing to deal with. I'd never been able to handle them very well and right now is nothing different. The moment Rage guided me into the main room of the clubhouse, I couldn't begin to process everything going through my head. At least not right then.

Now as I sit here with my best friends, a sense of relief washes over me. Here I thought the three of the most amazing women I've ever known would be pissed at me for leaving the way I did, instead, they all hugged me close, crying at seeing me again. The hard part about seeing them is finding out Kenny and Izzy are both pregnant. The news hit me right in the chest, but I'm happy for them. All of them.

"Cleo, you gotta tell us, did Rage really carry you out of Stoney's club, as Momma B said?" Izzy asks giggling, pulling me out of my head. I can't help but roll my eyes at her question.

"He did, much against my will," I mutter. Rage has a way of getting what he wants one way or another.

"Well, I for one am glad he finally brought your ass back here," Kenny says.

"Me too. I've missed you so much," Lynsdey speaks up. Out of all three of them, she's been mostly silent.

"You know, even though I didn't think I was ready to come home yet, I'm glad to be home. I've missed you guys as well. I'm sorry I left like that," I murmur not looking them in the eye.

"Cleo, we're here for you. I totally get it why you took off. Kenny and I might not know all of it and I'm sure Lynsdey doesn't even know the full story. However, when you want someone to talk to, we're here. That's what best friends are for, right?" Izzy asks that last part as she grips my wrist comfortingly.

"Izzy's right," Lynsdey whispers tears running down her cheeks. "You need to know how sorry I am you ended up being mixed up in my shit yet again. I blame myself for what you went through."

Lynsdey and I never really spoke about what Jake did to either of us in the past except for the basics. I know more of what he'd done to her then she does of me. I didn't want her to ever feel this guilt. I feel like a complete, selfish bitch right now for letting her think she was to blame. She never was. The blame needs to be laid where it's always supposed to have been, with Jake.

"Lyns, you're like my fuckin' sister, woman. You have nothing to be sorry about. None of this is on you. It never has been. By you thinking that it's your fault, Jake wins, even from the grave. How about we both put that day behind us and start healing. I know I need to. And maybe one day, I'll have the courage to tell you guys everything that happened but for now, I can't, it's still too much. I'd prefer to simply lock it away in a box and never open it again," I say, looking from Lynsdey to Kenny and Izzy.

"Sounds good to me. When you're ready, we'll be sure to do it somewhere that we can sit on a couch with lots of Blue Bell Dutch Chocolate ice cream and tequila for you to spill your heart out. Now, how about you tell us what you wanna do now that your back." That's Kenny for you. Always one for trying to make everything better.

"Oh, you should help me. I'm working on flipping my first house but I'm also working on organizing the first charity event for Letters from Above. I could use some help with it. The guys are doing a poker run for anyone who wants to join in. There's also gonna be a small carnival type thing followed by a concert with local talent. Demons Among Us have agreed to be a part of it." Izzy's eyes light up as she goes about telling me everything she's doing and what the cause is for. I think what she's doing is amazingly beautiful.

"Whatever I can do to help, I'm in," I say.

"Yay, if you want to help me with the concert part that would be great. I swear some people think they're talented but aren't. They need some sense of direction. And on top of that, you have the most beautiful voice there is when you sing." I groan at realizing what she's asking me to do. Ugh, I could bang my head on the table right now.

"Izzy, I haven't danced in a really long time, let alone sung. I really don't know if I could do that," I mutter.

"Oh, please, Cleo, you're the best dancer I've ever seen. Hell, you're the one that helped me put the choreography together for the waitresses. You could do it," Kenny says. Well, shoot a duck in the head, why don't you. Of course, she'd throw that out there.

"Izzy has all of us doing something to help out. I'm working on organizing vendors for the carnival. This event is going to be huge with all the help this woman has recruited. She's not only got the brothers from this club, but Stoney and Hammer's clubs are in on helping as well as the guys from SoCo Security," Lynsdey says, throwing her arms up dramatically.

"Well, what can I say? I want this to be perfect and we only have three months left. We have everything working out great except for the concert part. I feel like there's something missing from it. Something that would make it even more meaningful," Izzy mutters almost as if she were talking to herself.

For the better of an hour, we talk and joke, and everything seems to be going great even when the clubwhores keep eyeballin' me. It isn't until Cristy comes in that the atmosphere changes. She is pissed from the look on her face.

"Who the fuck do you think you are?" she asks with enough venom in her voice you can taste it.

"Excuse me?" I say in confusion. Looking at the rest of the girls, none of them meet my eyes.

"Excuse me? Seriously? Are you going to sit there and think you can just waltz right back into town and everything will go back to normal?" Cristy yells, placing her hands on her hips. I've never seen her as angry as she is right now.

"Cristy, if I've done something to you, I'm sorry, but you have no right to act like this toward me. I left for a reason. Now I'm back and I'm happy to see everyone, including you," I tell her as I stand. I've never been one to allow anyone to yell or scream in my face. I'm not about to let it start now.

"That's a good one. If you're so happy to see me along with everyone else, why didn't you call or even text? We're supposed to be your friends and you pushed us all aside like we're nothing but a sack of flour. You selfish bitch, you should be sorry," Cristy continues to rant.

"That's enough, Cristy," Kenny says from behind me. I didn't even realize I'd moved in front of the table.

"Oh, please, you can't tell me you're not pissed about her up and leaving without even giving you notice at the bar," Cristy snaps.

"Cristy, stop being a bitch," Lynsdey snaps. "You're just pissed over the fact Rage never gave you the time of day even while Cleo was gone."

"What?" I whisper.

"This has nothing to do with Rage. This is about the fact my supposedly good friend just ups and leaves us all without even a fuck you," Cristy says, getting in my face. "As for Rage, I'm sure he would have come around eventually. There's only so long a man can go without getting his dick wet."

I barely let Cristy finish her words before I'm on her, slamming my fist in her face over and over. Tears fill my eyes as I take all my aggression out on her. Punch after punch, I slam my fist into her until someone lifts me backward off of her.

"You bitch. You have no clue what the fuck you're talking about. You say we were friends. We never were if you talk shit like that to anyone. I left because I couldn't stand being around here seeing all my friends happy when I wasn't. I couldn't stand to see my own best friends living happily with newborn babies when I'd lost mine. I left to get better. Am I? No, I'm not, but I'm fucking trying. I don't need your shit.

"You want a man that doesn't want you, not my fuckin' fault. Just like it's not my fault that I was targeted, raped, tortured, and you don't want to know what else that sick bastard did to me. You want to call me selfish, that's okay, I'll be selfish for attempting to take my life. But I didn't because Stoney stopped me. However, it wasn't as simple as Stoney taking the knife from my hand. It was his words. So, I'm selfish for needing time. Now go fuck yourself. I don't want or need you to be my friend," I scream, not realizing the audience around the room or the fact I'm being held against a brick wall of a chest.

"I'm sorry, Cleo, I am," Cristy says, standing up with the help of one of the prospects. She may say the words, but I honestly don't believe her. No one says hateful things without meaning them. No, she's merely apologizing to save her ass from Rage and other club members.

"I think you need to leave, Cristy, and take some time off at the bar. Get your head on right," Rage says from behind me. I watch as Ace helps Cristy out the door.

Closing my eyes, I turn in his arms laying my head against

his chest. "Please tell me I didn't just have a full-blown meltdown in front of the entire club," I murmur.

"Can't tell you that, babe," Rage mutters, placing a kiss on the top of my head. "Let me see your hands."

Shaking my head, I pull back enough to look at him. At the tight lines on his face, I don't have to take a guess at him being pissed.

"I'm sorry, I shouldn't have done that," I whisper before turning to face the rest of the room. My eyes landing on one of my three best friends, seeing exactly what I didn't want. Pity. Unable to say anything to them or even turn back to Rage, I look down. "Can you take me home now, Rage?" I ask.

"Yeah, baby, let's get you home," Rage says, taking my hand.

There's a saying— one step forward, two steps back. And tonight, I not only took that first step forward, but I also took ten steps back. I feel emotionally drained. I never intended for any of that to happen. At least now I don't have to worry about them ever finding out or asking me to tell them. They already know.

# CHAPTER THIRTEEN

## RAGE

Fuckin' hell, I never expected to walk into the main room of the clubhouse to find my woman beating the shit out of another woman. Especially a woman who was supposed to be her friend. Lifting her off of Cristy, I wonder what set Cleo off. Didn't take long to find out when she started screaming, yelling at Cristy, pretty much informing the entire club of what happened that night. Good thing I'd already told my brothers about the baby. I wish I could erase the agony that filled my woman's voice as she spoke of that night and how it wasn't her fault.

I wanted nothing more than to strangle Cristy. She's a nice woman for the most part, even if a little infatuated with me.

The moment we got home, Cleo walked upstairs without saying a word. I don't want to give her too much time alone, afraid she'll sink back into her own head, after only just having her start to open up. I make sure the house is locked up before heading upstairs.

Walking into the bedroom, the sound of water running in the en suite bathroom grabs my attention. The thought of her in there alone hits me right in the chest. Without thinking, I open the door to find her sitting in the tub, rocking back and forth. Stripping out of my clothes, I climb in the scalding hot water, sitting behind her. I turn the water off before it can fill more than a couple inches. The last thing she needs is to fuck up the tattoo she got yesterday. Neither of us says a word as I pull her against my chest. Running my fingers along her arms, I wait for her to speak up.

"I'm sorry," Cleo whispers.

"Babe, you got nothing to be sorry about. Want to tell me what happened to set you off?"

"Not really, it's childish thinking about it now."

"For you to have gone off the way you did tonight, Lave, it had to have been something more than childish," I say, kissing the top of Cleo's head, hoping for her to tell me. I can't fix it if I don't know what happened. I hate seeing her in pain, emotionally or physically.

"Cristy came in pissed, calling me selfish for taking off the way I did and not staying in touch. She didn't even let me explain. I'm sure she doesn't know everything or she did and wanted to give me a hard time. We've all been friends for a long time even though the past few years, she's pulled away from all of us," Cleo says, pausing to take a breath. "What set me off though was when she said you wouldn't be able to go forever without getting your dick wet. It was like something took over my body and I went off on her. I mean, I get you're a man. Men have needs, just like women do. I wouldn't have held it against you if you couldn't be with me and me alone knowing I might not be able to give you everything you need."

I don't have to see her face to know she's crying; the trembling of her body says it all.

The fact is Cleo's own friend, whether she knows what happened or not, should never have attacked my woman. As much as it makes me damn proud to know she can defend herself when it comes to someone verbally abusing her, it never should've come to that. I don't give a flying fuck what I gotta do but Cristy isn't getting close to my woman again. Not fuckin' happenin'.

"Babe, when it comes to me and you, you've got nothing to worry about. We're solid, always have been. Since I first laid eyes on you, I haven't touched another woman or even wanted to. My dick doesn't get wet unless it's by you. In my eyes, Cleo, you are all I see," I murmur ,placing kisses on top of her head.

"I don't think I'll ever be the woman you first met again. She died the day our baby died," she says in a hushed whisper.

Turning her in my arms, I lift her chin so she has no choice but to look in my eyes. "Cleo, you are the woman I first met. You might not feel like it right now, but you are. She didn't die that day, she's simply in pain at the loss of something she couldn't control. You are my beautiful Lavender, don't forget it. Day by day, you will realize it for yourself as you heal." Her eyes are shimmering with tears as they fall down her cheeks. "Stop crying, babe, it kills me seeing you like this," I say, wiping her tears away.

"Thank you."

"Anytime, Lave, you know that. Now, let's get out of the tub and dry off so I can put you to bed," I tell her at the same time I begin to stand, bringing her with me.

Stepping out of the tub, I grab one of the towels hanging on the back of the door. Seeing Cleo for the first time naked in months, I bite the inside of my cheek to keep from groaning. She's the most beautiful woman I've ever seen. Taking my time, I dry her, soaking in every inch of her body. When I get to her stomach and thighs, I suck in a deep breath at the sight of scars there. Fuck, these look worse than the ones on her back.

Cleo attempts to turn away, but I stop her. Leaning forward, I place a kiss on each scar, gently letting her know they're nothing to be ashamed of. When she's ready and if she wants to, I'll take her to get them covered as well. With everything she's been through, she shouldn't have to suffer looking at these every day. To me, they mean she survived hell but I never want her to have to think of what happened to her ever again.

Standing back up, I pull her into our room, leading her to the bed and not bothering to put clothes on. I don't want any clothes between us right now. I need to hold her in my arms with nothing between us. No barriers to keep her body from touching mine. I'm thankful she doesn't protest my unspoken request. Cleo might not realize it right now, but even though she's hurting, she's still in tune with me. Same as she's always been. Always will be.

My woman's stronger than she realizes and I intend to show her.

Day by day.

# CHAPTER **FOURTEEN**

## CLEO

Over the last few weeks, I like to believe I've made some major improvements in moving on with my life. After the meltdown at the clubhouse, I didn't know how I'd be able to face any of them again. I'd tried to hole-up in the house, refusing to leave. However, that didn't stop everyone from coming to me. My friends along with different members of the club. The only one who didn't come by the house was Cristy. Which I'm grateful for, I'm not ready to face her yet.

Two days after the shitshow, Izzy came over carrying a bottle of my all-time favorite— apple pie moonshine. You can't get anything like this at the liquor store. Nope, we go through one of the regulars at the bar to get this. He makes it himself and it's the best damn moonshine in the area.

That day, Izzy confided in me everything she'd been through, let me know I'm not alone when it comes to grief. My heart broke for Izzy when she told me how she'd blamed herself for the death of her brother and how she attempted to take her own life. The only reason she's still here is because of

Twister. He saved her from making the biggest mistake of her life.

Shortly after Izzy and I started talking, both Kenny and Lynsdey showed up, bringing even more moonshine.

"We figured after the other night you could really use some of Bobby Joe's good stuff." Kenny smiled handing me the jar in her hand. I couldn't help but smile back. As humiliated as I'd been, these three women know me almost as well as Rage does.

The three of us spent the rest of the day sitting in the living room where Kenny and Lynsdey both shared everything that they'd been through in detail just as Izzy did. When they were done, I poured my heart out, telling them every gory detail. Telling my best friends, knowing they won't judge me, feels free.

Rage and I seemed to get into a routine as well. Especially when I started working at the garage. I didn't think I'd like working around a bunch of men considering everything, however, everyone has been nothing but nice toward me. The first couple of days in the garage, I spent the entire time organizing the haphazard stacks of papers mixed together with parts strewn around the office. How anyone could find anything amazes me still.

With each day, I've begun to feel like myself again, other than I still refuse to look in a mirror. Yesterday, the girls came into the shop looking like they were on a mission. I didn't know what they were up to until I was being dragged out of the office and into a car where they declared enough was enough. We spent the entire afternoon at our friend Emerson's salon. She's the only one I've ever trusted to do my hair and when she saw the state of it, you would've thought I was wearing a clown mask the way she screeched, demanding that I never abandon my sacred duty in keeping my hair done properly.

After apologizing and promising to take better care of my hair, she finally went to work on fixing the color and even gave me a hairstyle. I'd always worn my hair long, well past my shoulder blades, but I needed a change. Emerson ended up giving me a long bob which I think looks amazing. I didn't want to look in the mirror but when I did, I'd been amazed at the transformation. Rage even seemed to like my hair considering the look he gave me when I got home last night.

Rage has been nothing but supportive, encouraging me to do what makes me happy. Every day after work, we've spent the time together talking, whether it is something simple or not. He's listened and responded in ways I never imagined he would. Rage has shown me affection with each light touch and kiss to my forehead. With each gentle caress, I long for more. I don't know if I'm ready for sex just yet though at the same time, my body yearns for Rage's touch. Lying in bed with him holding me close every night doesn't seem to help either—especially considering when I wake up in the morning with his dick pressed into my ass. You'd think I'd shrink away from him not push closer, enjoying the feel of his entire body close to mine.

This morning was no different, well, all except for the fact I woke up alone. Usually, I wake up before him. Always have. Running my hand along his side of the bed, the sheets are cool to touch. Weird.

Getting out of bed, I do my thing in the bathroom before going to look for Rage. As I make my way past the guest room, the sound of a groan catches my attention, and the door is still partially opened. Curiosity beats me as I peek inside, finding Rage. I cover my mouth to keep him from hearing me gasp at what he's doing. His eyes are closed as his hand slides up and down his dick. I lick my lips nervously as I can't seem to tear my eyes from him masturbating. My eyes widen as he groans my name, pumping his hand even harder, spraying his stomach with cum. On one hand, I feel like an intruder for watching him, but at the same time, I'm completely aroused at knowing I'm the one he is thinking about.

I quickly step away not wanting to be caught watching him

only to back right into the wall behind me. At the thud of my head hitting the wall, Rage appears in front of me standing there in nothing but his boxers. At least he had enough time to pull his boxers up, I think to myself. Oh God, if he realizes I caught him taking care of himself, I don't think I could face him. Hell, it's hard enough right this minute standing in front of him when all I want to do is take care of my own needs or better yet, have Rage help me.

"You okay, babe?" he says, coming closer.

"Umm yeah, I'm okay, sorry, I'm just heading to the kitchen," I mutter, not making eye contact.

"You sure?" Rage lifts my face up to look at him.

From the smirk on his face, I say there's no denying the fact he knows I'd seen him.

I'm busted. Damn, llama spit on a stick.

"Umm yeah, I could really use some coffee. Then I think I might go outside and work on the flowerbeds, they're a mess. We could really do with a new border and mulch in them," I spout on trying to change the direction of our conversation.

"We can do that, babe," Rage says, smiling.

"Oh, you don't have to help, I can do it. I'm sure you have plenty that needs to get done."

"Cleo, you're not doing shit outside by yourself. Not when you have to use tools or shit like that."

"Excuse me?" I ask, narrowing my eyes at him in irritation.

"Babe, I don't care what you do around the house except for if tools are needed, that's my department. I don't go fucking with shit in the kitchen cause that's your domain and you told me a long time ago to stay out of your way, otherwise, you'd deny me dessert. Well, I'll tell you the same thing. Fuck with shit that needs tools, you won't get dessert," Rage grumbles as he pulls me flush against his chest. "And when I say dessert, I'm not talking about chocolate cake."

I'm speechless as Rage releases me, taking a step back. Taking a deep breath to clear my head, I finally manage to find my voice. "Don't you dare try pulling some he-man, alpha card with me. I can work in the yard, same as you."

"I know you can but doesn't mean I'm not gonna help you." Rage grabs one of my hands. "As for the he-man, alpha card bullshit, this isn't me doing none of that shit. If I were, you'd know in a heartbeat. What I'm saying is I don't want these smooth hands calloused by working with a bunch of tools. You can work on the flowerbeds, pull the fuckin' weeds out, do whatever you want but when it comes to doing anything else, babe, I'll handle that shit. Now, stop fussing with me over this otherwise we won't be doing fuck at all outside and I'll take you to bed and turn your ass red."

"Fine, I'll let you handle whatever just stay out of my way," I throw over my shoulder gaining his laughter in the process.

I need to get my head on straight. My body is practically shaking with need for him, but can I have him without being reminded of what Jake did to me. I want to, God knows I do, maybe I should take the plunge and go for it.

# CHAPTER **FIFTEEN**

## RAGE

"Lave, you can't use those that fuckin' way, you'll end up chopping your damn toes off. Hell, you shouldn't even be out here working on the yard barefoot as it is," I growl pulling the shears out of Cleo's hands. While I was cutting the grass, I'd looked up to find her taking my hedge trimmers to one of the bushes. Getting off the mower, I rushed over to keep her from doing any more damage, the bush was already in shambles from her attempting to shape it.

"Stop exaggerating, I wasn't going to cut my toes off," she gripes wiping sweat off her forehead.

"You were close enough, babe. Fuck, what are you doing with these anyway? I told you already, don't touch the tools, I'll handle that part," I ask, irritated she didn't listen to me.

"I needed these bushes trimmed up in order to get around them."

"Trimmed up, really, babe? You realize this isn't trimmed. You mutilated this bush," grumbling I point to the bush.

"Maybe I was trying to take it down so I can put some flowers here. There are too many bushes as it is."

"Lave, I love you, however, if you touch another one of my tools, I won't stop myself from taking you over my knee. You hear me?" I bark pissed she doesn't get the fact she could've hurt herself.

Doesn't help my dick is hard as a rock and has been since I saw her watching me jerk off this morning. I'd woken up to her rubbing her ass against my dick in her sleep, but knowing she's not ready for me to take her yet, I'd gotten out of bed. I'd gone to the guest room to take care of myself. I'd heard her out in the hall as I had been getting close. When I'd seen her out of the corner of my eye, I couldn't stop myself from coming if I'd wanted to. Her eyes had filled with lust as she kept her eyes on my dick.

Shaking my head, I turn, leaving her standing there without another word and taking the trimmers with me. I need to get away from her before I do what I want and take her right here in the yard. Not saying I'd force her even if I know her body wants mine as much as mine wants hers. When I have her again, I'm gonna hear the words.

After putting the trimmers down next to the mower, I get back to cutting the grass. Glancing over to Cleo, I groan at the fact she's now kneeling in the damn flower bed pulling weeds. Her back on display in that damn tank top showing off part of the tattoo Burner finished up for her. It turned out perfect, with a woman surround by spiritual animals, but what gets me every time I get a glance of it are the woman's eyes. I don't know how else to explain it other than they're something majestic about them.

Fuck, my dick is gonna break off before all is said and done with if I continue on like this.

---

By the time we finish working on the yard, it is close to dinner time. Neither of us spoke after our spout earlier. Before, whenever Cleo would piss me off, I'd take her to bed, fuck her until she realized the error of her ways. Now though, I'm not sure of how to handle it.

"I'm gonna shower and fix dinner. Would you grill the steaks for me if I do the rest?" Cleo asks as we both walk inside.

"Yeah," I grunt in response, heading to the refrigerator and grabbing a beer. My answer must've worked for her since she doesn't respond but heads to the bedroom. Fuck, I want to be able to join her in there. Maybe I need to head over to the club for a few hours, cool down some before I rush her into something she's not ready for.

Deciding that's a good idea, I go grab my clothes out of the room, hurrying as to not be tempted to join her. Jumping in the guest shower, I make it fast in order to get out of here before she's done with her own. I'll leave a note saying I got called out for club business. I hate lying to her but if I don't leave and cool down some, I'm afraid I'll end up doing something stupid.

Turning off the shower, I listen out for Cleo while putting my clothes on. I can hear the shower in our bathroom still on. Going into the kitchen, I write her a note letting her know I'd gone to the clubhouse and if she needs me to call. With that done, I head to my bike. Turning the key, the roar she gives me sends a relief down my spine. My bike has always been like an extension of me, giving me the freedom I need with riding.

Turning out of the driveway, I hope by leaving for a little while, I've made the right decision. Either way, I'll find out later when I get back home.

Pulling up to the clubhouse, I park my bike next to Thorn's, surprised he's here on a Saturday night. Usually, he's at home with his ol' lady and kids. Walking inside, I find him sitting at the bar holding a picture in his hand while drinking his beer.

Furrowing my brow, I take a seat next to him. "What's going on with you, brother?" I ask nodding to Ace to give me a beer.

"Trying to figure out something that's been bugging the shit out of me for a while now," he mutters putting the picture down on the bar.

"Wanna talk about it?"

"After the shit went down with Lynsdey and Cleo, Bishop's dad gave Lyns this album of old photos. I took a picture of it when I first saw it and sent it to Gadget. One of the couples is Lyns parents. What gets me is the other couple, I recognized them but couldn't put my finger on it at first. Now, I know who it is and I'm not sure how to approach it. I don't even think Bishop knows this."

"What's that?"

"Hades is Lyns's family," Thorn says loud enough for only my ears, showing me the picture. I stare at it, dumbfounded. Holy shit, the man Thorn is referring to is Hades' dad. The one that had been killed.

"How are they related? I don't get it. Bishop's dad is Lynsdey's uncle?" This shit is confusing as fuck.

"My guess is Hades' mom is related to Lynsdey's mom and crazy aunt."

"It makes sense, the aunt was a part of that cult. You need to show this to Hades, man. There's no way around it. They all have a right to know," I say placing a hand on his shoulder.

"Your right, man I'll bring it up at church tomorrow."

"Good idea, Thorn, least he will have his brothers to lean on when he finds out he's got family here," I say in agreement.

"Anyways, what are you doing here? Figured you'd be at home with Cleo."

"Needed some time to myself," I mutter, not wanting to get into the fact I'm sexually frustrated. The last thing I need is to have my brothers making jokes about my dick. Knowing them, they'd say some shit about me meeting Pamela and her five friends or some shit like that.

"You sure, man?"

"What the fuck you two fuckers doing here looking like

bitches sulking?" Horse asks from behind me. Fuck, I didn't hear him walk up to us.

"I should ask you the same thing, VP." I smirk at him. He's the same as Thorn and usually at home with Kenny and JC.

"Shit, Kenny's in one of her moods. I swear she was never this cranky when she was carrying JC," Horse grumbles sitting down on my other side. "What's that?" he asks, pointing at the picture still in my hand as he grabs the beer placed in front of him.

"Nothing important right now. I just know I'll be bringing something to the clubs attention tomorrow, and it might be a hard pill to swallow when I say what I gotta say," Thorn says, taking the picture from my hand.

"This got anything to do with the shit your women went through?" Horse calmly asks without pushing for more.

"Something like that," Thorn mutters, finishing off his beer before standing up. "I need to head home to my woman and the kids. See you assholes tomorrow," he says dryly.

Turning my back to the bar, I look around the club. Saturday is usually a wild night and as my brothers continue to drink, they won't care what the fuck they do in front of each other.

"Wanna shoot a game of pool?" Horse asks breaking the silence between us.

"Yeah, sounds good. Want to see if Gadget and Dragon want to play teams?" I smirk, eyeing the twins over at the pool table getting ready to start again.

"Fuck yeah, put a hundred on if I tell them Dr. Connors' is helping the girls, they start fucking up their game."

"You're on." Laughing, we make our way to our brothers, ready to fuck with them. This is what I need to get my mind off the tension at home. Spending time with my brothers.

Two games in and I'm handing Horse a hundred-dollar bill, shaking my head. Gadget and Dragon are fucked when it comes to the pretty little doctor. I don't know what the story is with the three of them, but I know from the expressions they both have whenever her name is mentioned, they're head over heels for her. We all know when it comes down to them settling down, it won't be with separate women but one special one. They deserve it. Same as all my brothers. I hope one day, they all find the woman they deserve.

Pulling out my phone to check the time, I realize I've missed a call from Cleo. Fuck. Hitting the call back button, it rings until going to voicemail. Figuring she's gone to sleep, I agree to play one more game of pool then head home.

Hopefully, she won't be completely pissed with me.

# CHAPTER **SIXTEEN**

## CLEO

I shouldn't have been surprised when I got out of the shower to find Rage gone. His note really shouldn't have pissed me off, but it did. I was wound up fuckin' tight after watching him all day while we worked on the yard. When he fussed at me earlier, I'd been working on trimming the bushes. I knew what I was doing, I'm not a dumbass who doesn't know how to work with tools. However, he'd distracted me by coming around the side of the house shirtless on the mower. All I could think about was seeing him earlier in the morning taking care of himself and I hacked the bush to pieces coming close to my feet as I put the trimmers into the dirt.

After he walked away, taking the trimmers from me, he didn't say another word to me throughout the rest of the day. Hell, he barely answered me when I asked if he'd grill the steaks for me.

Right now, I don't know how to handle him leaving the way he did without saying anything. His note said "club business" which I'm pretty sure is a load of horseshit. I'd planned for us to have a nice dinner together, but you know what, fuck it. If he can go out to the clubhouse, then I can go out all the same.

I message the girls really quick to see if any of them are busy tonight. Kenny and Lynsdey both been home alone as well with their kids, but Izzy agreed to meet me at Outlaw Racks. This will be the first time I step foot in there since being back. Going up to our room, I quickly change into a pair of jeans and tank top and throw my hair up into a messy bun.

Making my way to the door, I grab the keys to Rage's truck along with my purse, locking the house behind me. I've never driven his truck; it's one of his babies along with his bike. However, I don't have a car yet, so he'll have to get over it when he finds out. When I get enough money saved, I'll get my own ride, maybe a cherry red Dodge Ram. I've always thought they were hot.

Cranking up the radio, Bulletproof by Godsmack blaring, I make my way to the bar, pulling up at the same time as Izzy, not missing the fact Twister is with her. Of course, he wouldn't let her out without him. Not with it being a Saturday at Outlaws. It's always packed with a live band, usually Demons Among Us.

"Where's Rage?" Izzy asks as I climb out of the truck.

"According to his note, he was needed at the clubhouse for club business. Which I figured was bullshit before, but now I know for sure he lied seeing Twister here," I say sarcastically, looking in Twister's direction.

"What the hell? Why the hell did he do that shit?" Izzy asks as we walk inside.

"I don't know, maybe it's because I caught him this morning jerking off or the fact I didn't listen to him when he told me not to touch the yard tools. All I know is he lied, and I can't help wondering if he's gone to the club to let someone else take care of him."

"You really think that?" Izzy's brows furrow in concern.

"Maybe, I don't know. I mean, it's not like we do anything

intimate." Shrugging my shoulders, I look away from her, taking the bar in as we make our way to a table. I smile at the fact that nothing's changed. Why I thought it would, I'm not sure, but I'm glad it hasn't.

"Cleo, there's no way that man would ever look in another woman's direction, not with the way he feels about you. You weren't there to see how messed up he was after the shit fest you and Lynsdey went through. He was a mess, it fucked with his head. I may not have known what was going through his head, but I can tell you from the look in his eyes, he wasn't in a good place. If he didn't love you, he could've been with anyone, but still he didn't, he never once strayed from you while you two were separated. He may have fucked up back then by not staying by your side, but his head and heart were at war with each other. Just think of that. If he couldn't stray from you then, why would he go look for someone now that he has you at home," Izzy says, keeping her eyes on mine.

We sit there listening to the band play for a few minutes as I take in what she's told me. Am I simply being insecure due to everything? Looking around the bar, I spot Cristy working. Catching her eye, she gives me a knowing smirk at the fact Rage isn't with me.

"I thought Cristy wasn't working here anymore," I ask, looking back at Izzy, who then looks toward her man, who was sitting at another table with Hades and Burner, all three of them looking our way. Turning back to Izzy, I wait for an answer. I end up having to clear my throat to gain her attention.

"Sorry." Izzy turns her attention back to me, laughing. "Everyone wanted to tell her to kick rocks. Unfortunately, we can't due to employee regulations. Kenny's chomping at the bit to fire her for the shit she said to you, but since it didn't happen here, she can't, otherwise it could be a lawsuit against the bar."

"Oh, well, that sucks. I mean, I don't want her to lose her job over something like her and I getting into it. No one should lose their income over something so petty," I mutter, waving over our waitress and finally ordering a drink, sticking to soda since I'm driving.

"I get what you mean, still, Cristy was supposed to be our friend and for her to say what she did was beyond fucked up," Izzy says, narrowing her eyes toward the bar.

"Do you think she still has a thing for Rage?" I ask more to myself than anything.

"I honestly don't know. I mean, she never said anything about being interested in him, and I didn't even know about her having a thing for him 'til Lyns threw it out there."

"Neither did I really. Cristy never said anything to me when we hung out nor did she act strange when the guys were around us. I don't know, I'm so confused about everything. I want to make amends with her even if she's done with me," I say, looking down at the table, unsure of the mess going around in my head. Even weeks later, I can still hear Cristy's words about Rage running around in my head and him leaving the house the way he did doesn't help.

"You know we have your back if you want to try to work things out with her, but if I were you, I'd wait for her to come to you. She's the one that fucked up, not you. Now, back to what we originally came here for, you and Rage are sexually frustrated and need to just get it out of the way," Izzy smirks at me.

"I want to, God knows I do, I'm just scared," I whisper.

"What's there to be scared about, Cleo?" Izzy asks, lifting a brow at my statement.

"Everything," I say, looking away, ashamed.

"Cleo, listen to me. When it comes to that man, as I said earlier, you have nothing to worry about as far as him wanting you. It's all in your head. Let your body and heart take the wheel for a while," Izzy murmurs, pointing from my head to my heart. "Who knows, you might find you like it way better than being stuck in your head all the time."

Sitting forward, balancing my chin on my hands, I take in Izzy's advice. Do I say screw it and let my heart and body have control or stay in my head? I want nothing more than to move forward with my life, including being with Rage— in every way possible.

"You're right. I need to get out of my head. At least somewhat," I breathe out.

"More than somewhat," Izzy says, squinting her eyes at me. "Don't pressure yourself, Cleo. Simply be you and let things happen. Don't force them to happen before they're supposed to."

"Okay," I say in agreement. "How about we dance, have some fun while we're here." Standing up, I make my way to the dance floor.

Izzy and I spend the rest of the night having a blast dancing with each other. Anytime some random guy would try getting our attention, they learned quickly to back away. The two of us simply shook our heads at Twister and the other two guys as they stationed themselves at the edge of the dance floor. The night was a blast, even at the end of it when Izzy and I parted ways, her and Twister heading back to the clubhouse where they're staying until their house is ready. I head home with Hades and Burner following to make sure I get home.

Getting home, I notice Rage still isn't here. Trying not to let it bother me, I head inside, locking the door behind me. I don't know what will happen between the two of us, but I'm determined to take Izzy's advice to go with the flow.

Pulling out my phone, I call Rage to let him know that I'm home after spending time with Izzy at the bar only to get his voicemail. I'm sure he's just having fun, even if my mind wants to say he's doing something otherwise.

Determined not to let it get to me, I strip out of my clothes and climb into bed. Closing my eyes, I fall asleep to visions of Cristy and Rage, Rage and other women, and women sneering at me as they take the man I love.

# CHAPTER SEVENTEEN

## RAGE

Horse and I are just finishing up our last game of pool when the slamming of the front door draws my attention. Looking up, I find myself under the scrutiny of Izzy's ice stare. What the hell did I do to her? When she makes a move to head in my direction, Twister stops her, sending her off in the opposite direction. Once Izzy leaves the room, Twister comes over to where Horse and I are.

"What's up, Prez?" I ask curiously, wondering why I got that icy stare from his woman.

"Rage, I swear, I love you like my own flesh and blood, but I want nothing more than to beat the ever-lovin'-fuck out of you right now," Twister growls, swiping a hand through his hair.

"What the fuck did I do to piss you off?" I ask in surprise. Far as I know, I've done everything I'm supposed to have done.

"It's not me you pissed off, it's my woman. 'Cause of your stupid ass, I had to spend the night not wrapped around my woman like I wanted but at Outlaw Racks keeping men away from her and Cleo while they danced and had fun. You think I want my pregnant woman at a bar full of drunk as fuck men?" Twister yells in my face.

Stepping back, I blink in astonishment. Here I thought I'd come here to relax away from Cleo only to find out she decided to up and go party somewhere drunk fucks would hit on her. Fuck that. Without saying a word to anyone, I throw the pool stick down on the table and head for the door. If Cleo thinks she can get away with this shit, she's dead wrong.

"Where the fuck you goin'?" Hades yells out over the sound of his bike as he parks next to my own bike.

"Home," I growl out.

"Good, we made sure she got there safe and sound. Take it easy on her, brother, you didn't see the defeated look in her eyes like we did," he tells me as he turns his bike off.

"What do you mean?" I ask, furrowing my brows.

"Means she's lost in that head of hers and I don't know if you can pull her out of it. It doesn't take her talking to me to know where her mind was. You left her at the house by herself to come to the clubhouse on a Saturday night, leaving her to sit alone thinking about what you could be doing."

Motherfucker, he's right. I fucked up big time with this. Blowing out a breath, I sit back on my bike, scrubbing my hands over my face.

"I don't know what to do, brother. I fuckin' want her, all of her, but I'm not trying to rush her. I rush her and she'll hate me." Shaking my head, trying to clear it.

"You wouldn't be rushing her if you take the time to show her how much she means to you. The answer to your question is to *love* her, not *fuck* her," Hades says, patting my back as he moves toward the door.

Starting my bike up, I back out of my spot. Turning for home, I think of Hades' words. Cleo needs to be shown how much she means to me. I thought she knew she was my world. I've told her I love her, and I do. Guess the saying "actions speak louder than words" is right. I need to prove to her how much she means to me not only with words but with my body as well.

As I pull up to the house, the first thing I notice is how crooked my truck is parked. Shit, I didn't even think of her taking my truck. I've never let anyone drive my truck other than my dad when he brought her down here for me. She's a beast and I baby the fuck out of her, same as I do my bike. Taking a quick walk around her, making sure she didn't scratch my truck up, I decide I either need to teach her how to drive my girl properly or get her something smaller. I'd been meaning to take her to look, however, I've kept putting it off because I love her riding with me everywhere.

Walking into the house, I'm greeted by silence. I go through, making sure everything is locked and head toward the bedroom. I find her lying in the middle of the bed, her head going side to side, breathing hard. She must be having a nightmare. Discarding my clothes, I climb into the bed. Her body stiffens when I pull her against me.

"Rage?" she questions sleepily.

"Yeah, Lavender, it's me. Go back to sleep," I tell her, kissing the top of her head.

Rolling over to face me, Cleo looks up into my eyes, half dazed. "Make me your woman again, Rage," she whispers.

Did she just say what I think she did? I gotta be hearing things. "Go back to sleep, baby, we can talk in the morning."

"Please, Rage? I need to know I'm your woman. I can't go back to sleep without knowing. If you don't want me, I get it. I mean, look at me, my body isn't the same as it used to be. I'm flawed—"

I slam my mouth down on hers to keep her from finishing that sentence. Taking her to her back, I kiss her long and hard, only pulling away when we're both breathless.

"Lavender, you don't see you the way I do. I love everything about you. You're the only one I want in this bed next to me," I murmur between kisses along her jawline down to her neck. "You're beautiful."

I take my time kissing every inch of skin as I move down her body. Her nipples are hard as I make my way to them, grabbing one in one hand and sucking the other one into my mouth. Her moans are music to my ears. Cleo begins to wiggle underneath me as I use my free hand to slide between her legs while I give each of her breast attention.

The feel of Cleo's hands in my hair, pulling at it as I lavish her body, has my dick jerking. It's ready to explode as it is. Not having her for so long has him anxious to be inside her. He'll have to wait though until I've had my taste of her, needing to taste all of her, I move further down her body, lifting her legs over my shoulders.

"Tell me what you want, Lave," I order, breathing her in, loving the way she smells.

"I want you, Rage, all of you," Cleo moans out.

"That's not what I want to hear, baby. You know what I want to hear," I say hoarsely.

"I can't," she whispers apprehensively.

"You can," I tell her.

"Please," she begs.

"I'll give you what we both want, soon as you tell me," I say, running a finger down her slit.

"I want you to use your mouth on me, please, Rage," she finally says.

"Good girl. Here you go, baby. But next time, you use my name. My real name," I say before proceeding to take her pussy with my mouth, devouring her. Fuck, I've missed this. She's like tasting heaven. Using my fingers, I find the spot that sends her over as I latch onto her clit. Cleo's screams fill the room when she comes. Her body shaking as her pussy spasms around my fingers. I don't relent as I continue taking what I've wanted from the moment I brought her home.

"Please, no more. I need you inside me, Travis," Cleo moans

while writhing under me.

I don't say a word, needing the same thing, and since she used my name, I'll give it to her. "Say it again," I order, lining my dick up with her pussy, pressing in slightly only to pull away when she pushes for me to enter her.

"I need you," she whispers

"That's not it, baby."

"Travis, plea—" she cries out as I thrust home. Seated deep inside her, I stay still long enough for Cleo to adjust to my width. I'm not a small dude and don't want to hurt her.

Without words, she lets me know to move. Leaning over her, I take her mouth, loving the fact she doesn't have a problem with tasting herself as I kiss her. Thrusting slowly, I make love to my woman, showing her exactly how much she means to me.

"Travis," Cleo cries out, clenching my dick as she comes around me. Unable to hold back, I follow her, coming deep in her pussy.

"Fuck, I love you, Lavender. You're mine, always have been, always will be," I groan out.

"I love you too," she says breathlessly.

"I'm putting a ring on this finger, baby. I want you to marry me. No, I *need* you to marry me."

"W . . . what did you just say?" she stammers.

"I said I need you to marry me," I tell her between kisses.

"You need to marry me?" she asks, tears in her eyes.

"Yeah, Lavender, I do. I need you to marry me and become my family in every way possible."

"Yes," she says, nodding her head in agreement.

"Fuck, yeah, baby," I say and then proceed to show her how much she means to me for the rest of the night, lavishing her body, giving her and me everything we've been missing out on.

I'll spend the rest of my days showing her how much she means to me; fuck, I'll even find a way to give her everything she can't have anymore.

I'll give her the family she's always wanted.

# CHAPTER **EIGHTEEN**

## CLEO

Last night, I never expected Rage to ask me to marry him. Hell, I honestly thought he'd leave me when I asked him to make me his woman again. I'd been having a hard time sleeping when he'd gotten home, afraid my dreams were reality. Only when he climbed in next to me did I know what was real and what wasn't. I knew then and there what I wanted and needed.

Rage spent the entire night showing me exactly what I needed. Him. He's always been it for me, from day one. I should never have doubted him. My head can be one fucked up place to be. My heart and body know where they belong and after last night, my head finally knows as well.

Waking up this morning, I'm more than content to stay in his arms simply laying here enjoying the tranquility of the morning. Gently turning toward him, I take in his features like I've done so many times before only this time, he seems completely at peace. The tension which circled us finally gone.

Reaching up, I run my fingers along the scruff he keeps trimmed close to his face. I smile thinking of the life we'll have together. Doesn't mean I won't long for what we've lost, knowing I'll never be able to carry a child again. I like to think the beautiful child I lost before I even knew I'd carried was a little boy who'd have looked just like his daddy. My heart aches for our baby but I know I'll always carry him in my heart.

"What are you thinking so hard about, baby?" Rage's voice, filled with sleep, pulls me from my thoughts.

"I was just thinking of everything. How happy I am right now. Is it wrong to be so happy after having lost our child?"

"No, Lave, it's not wrong to be happy. It means you're healing. Doesn't mean you or I will forget about the child we never got to meet," he says, running his fingers through my hair, brushing it out of my face.

"You know when I think about the baby, I imagine a little boy who looks like his daddy." Tears fill my eyes as I admit it out loud to him.

"Yeah?"

"Yeah, it hurts to know we'll never have the chance to see that beautiful boy grow up. I always wanted a house full of kids. Growing up an only child, my parents always working, it was way too lonely. I know they loved me in their own way. They simply didn't know how to let it show. I wanted to do all the things my parents weren't able to do with me. You know I'm not close with them now, hell, I haven't even spoken to either of them in months. They never had time for me. I told myself I'd never do that to my own children. I'd never miss Trick or Treating, Thanksgiving, Christmas, or their birthdays. All the things my own parents missed out on," I say, letting the tears fall from my eyes. I've always hated crying yet, here I am constantly bawling like a baby recently.

Rage sits up, bringing me with him, holding me to his chest. Silently, he brushes away my tears. "Baby, I love you and I'd love nothing more than to have everything you just mentioned. I know I've said it before, and I'll tell you again. When you're ready, we'll find a way to start a family. If you want, we can talk to another doctor, find out the extent of damage, double-check about you or hell, look into our options of surrogates. We can keep our options open until we speak to someone. I also wouldn't mind adoption if that's the way we end up going. Doesn't matter to me as long as I'm doing it with you by my side," he says, proceeding to draw more tears out of me. Ugh, I wish I could stop crying.

Speechless, I lean forward kissing him, moaning as he sweeps his tongue into my mouth, taking over the kiss. Running my hands down his body, I find him hard and ready for me. Feeling bold, I straddle his waist, aligning myself with his dick. I sink down, taking him all the way in. The groan he makes spurs me on as I slowly begin to ride him. Rage grabs hold of my waist in a firm grip as he thrusts deep inside of me. Neither of us breaking eye contact as we connect, staring into each other's gaze. The only sound filling the room is our heavy breathing.

Growing closer to the edge of oblivion, Rage flips us over, thrusting even deeper inside with each movement of his hips. Seconds later, I scream out his name as the most powerful orgasm I've ever experienced hits me. Rage's groans fill my ears as he follows me into the bliss. His dick twitches as he stills, coming inside me.

"Fuck, baby, I could stay like this all day. Being inside you is the best place in the world." Rage groans, thrusting inside me, slowly drawing out the sensations.

"Same here, hot stuff," I moan out.

"Hot stuff? Seriously, sweetheart, I know I'm hot but damn." Smirking at me, he begins to tickle me.

"Well, mister, being hot, you might as well be called hot stuff," I say giggling.

"Oh, Lavender, baby, you can call me hot stuff all you want especially when I still have my dick deep in this pussy of yours." Rage smiles, leaning down and kissing me thoroughly before moving to stand by the bed. "Come shower with me," he says, holding his hand out to help me out of bed.

Smiling, I take his hand, letting him pull me the rest of the way. He kisses me deeply as he draws me flush against his body. Pulling back, he sweeps me off my feet, turns and heads toward our bathroom, not once putting me down to turn the shower on.

Taking his time, he washes my hair and body. Closing my eyes, I moan at the sensation of his hands exploring my skin.

When I open my eyes, I see nothing but pure adoration.

"Did you mean what you asked me last night?"

Rage cups my ass, drawing me against him as he graces me with the biggest smile I think I've ever seen. "Meant it, Lavender, you and me, I don't care if it's to the courthouse tomorrow or we wait a few weeks and have a small wedding here at the house, but I plan on having you as my wife. I want my name attached to yours as well as inked into this beautiful skin," he growls right before taking my mouth and body once more.

This day simply can't get any better than it already is.

# CHAPTER
# NINETEEN

## RAGE

"Come on, baby, we gotta get a move on or we're gonna be late," I yell out for Cleo to hurry up. It's been one hell of a week. Cleo decided she didn't want to do a wedding here at the house, settling with a courthouse wedding on one condition, my folks had to be here for it. That was it. She didn't care if anyone else came but my mom and dad. Said it was important they saw the two of us get married, especially my mom. I couldn't agree more.

They finally arrived last night, having been told we had an appointment set at the courthouse to be married today. Mom had been ecstatic, taking Cleo out, declaring she needed one on one time with my woman.

"I'm coming, geez, we're not gonna be late, Rage. I couldn't pick out which boots I wanted to wear," she grumbles coming down the hall looking absolutely mouthwatering. A simple white sundress matched with charcoal grey knee-high boots. The outfit suits her to a T.

"Fuck, Lave, I don't know if I can let you out of the house looking like that. Anyone sees you and I may end up stabbing them in the eyes to keep them from staring at you. You're beautiful, babe," I groan pulling her in for an appreciative kiss. "Let's go get married so I can bring my wife home and fuck her in these boots," I say squeezing her ass.

"Can't wait," she says, grinning.

---

"Can you believe this fucker up and got married on us?" Burner yells out later the same night as Cleo and I walk into the clubhouse for a cookout meant for us. Neither of us wanted a reception, however, my mom wouldn't hear of it.

"Fuck you, man." I grin, punching him in the chest. Nothing and no one could put me in a bad mood, not today at least.

After Cleo and I said our vows and signed the dotted line, I took her ass straight back to the house where I spent the afternoon enjoying every inch of her body. Not before I had her against the door with her dress hiked up and them hot as fuck boots wrapped around my waist.

"Shit, man, you didn't have to punch me in the damn chest that damn hard. Fuckin' hell, need to hold off on the steroids, especially now. Gotta make sure it doesn't shrivel up if you know what I mean," Burner chuckles as Cleo giggles by my side.

"What are you giggling about, babe?" I ask lifting a brow.

"I can't help it. The thought of you on steroids is hilarious. Can you imagine your arms any bigger? Even if you were on steroids, at least I don't have to worry about it affecting that part of your body. He's huge by himself," she giggles gliding her fingers along my abdomen.

"Damn right, he's huge. And I don't need fuckin' steroids to keep up with these guns. I got you for that and I plan to be working up a sweat with you again soon enough," I growl, pulling her against me so I can take her mouth, not giving a single fuck as to what anyone has to say. Catcalls and whistles surround us, and pulling back, both of us are breathless from the intensity of the kiss.

"Get a room you two," someone yells out from somewhere behind me.

"You about ready to head out of here, beautiful? I know I can't wait to get back between those sweet legs of yours," I ask giving her a smirk in the process.

"As much as I want to go home right this minute, I think the girls and your mom would kill both of us. They went to all this trouble putting this together for us, I'd hate to piss them off. I'm sure the lot of them could do damage if provoked." Cleo shutters as she finishes speaking.

Looking over her shoulder, I spot the women in which she'd just mentioned giving me the stink eye as if they knew I'd been trying to head out. I mean, shit, I did marry my woman this morning, it's our day and we can do what the fuck we want. Looking back at Cleo, I opened my mouth to say exactly that only to be shot down right away by all the damn women swarming around Cleo pushing me out of the way. Well damn, okay, then. Shaking my head, I move toward the bar needing a beer anyway.

"Don't you think you rushed into things a little too quickly, Rage?" a feminine voice asks from behind me. Turning around, I find Cristy standing way too close for my liking.

"What are you doing here, Cristy?" I grunt.

"Your mom invited me. Actually, she invited all the staff from the bar and Kenny okayed it. So here I am," Cristy answers, holding her arms out wide before twirling around as if it's not a big deal for her to be here.

"I think you need to leave," I suggest, knowing her being around my woman isn't a good idea. Not after Burner and Hades informed me of the way she kept giving the evil eye to Cleo when her and Izzy had been at Outlaw Racks a week ago.

I'm not about to let her hurt the woman I swore to always cherish and protect with my life mere hours ago.

"Why should I leave, I'm not doing anything wrong?" Cristy huffs, crossing her arms under her tits, almost pushing them out of the top she's got on.

"Hey, honey, what are you doing over here?" Cleo asks, sliding up next to me, wrapping her arms around my waist. "Oh, hey Cristy, I'm so glad you were able to come out tonight. I didn't think you'd be able to," my beautiful woman says all too sweetly. Inwardly grinning, I know what she's doing. I'd be doing the same thing if the tables were turned.

"Congrats, Cleo, I'm happy for you, I was just telling Rage the same," Cristy says in the same sweet manner Cleo used.

"Thank you. I've been meaning to apologize to you for what I did to your face that night, although thinking back on it, I'm not sorry," Cleo says, stepping out of my hold, standing toe to toe with Cristy. "Next time you want something, find it somewhere else. Now if you don't mind, I'd like you to leave. Oh, and don't bother showing up to work tomorrow, Kenny will simply be firing you. You can ask her if you want, though I'll go ahead and inform you of the fact I spoke with all the waitresses for Kenny the other day when I came by to see her and they've all told on you. You've been threatening them in order to get sixty percent of their tips. I, for one, would love to know what for, but right now, I don't care enough to find out. So, you can either walk out of here on your own or I'll have one of the brothers escort you out."

"Bitch, please, you know what I can't wait for? Rage to realize what a piece of shit you are. That's alright, I can wait a little while longer. I've waited this long as it is. He'll grow tired of your scarred-up body and go looking for someone who can give him what you can't," she says snidely before turning around and strutting away from us. I place a hand around Cleo's waist to keep her from going after the bitch. I'm not about to let some jealous cunt ruin our day. Nodding over to the prospect silently ordering him to follow Cristy out the gate.

"Come on, Lave, let's get back to having a good time," I murmur into Cleo's ear while holding her close to me.

"You know what, let's get out of here. After this bullshit, I want to end our wedding night on a good note, meaning I want you making love to me," Cleo whispers, wrapping her arms around my neck.

"Then what are we doing standing around here?" I ask, lifting her up and over my shoulder, carting her away from the party.

Time to get to it and show Cleo what it means to be my ol' lady.

# CHAPTER **TWENTY**

## CLEO

The last few months have been nothing but pure, unimaginative bliss since the day I made Rage my husband. His parents went back home a few days after the wedding. Unfortunately, Bear needed to get back to the clubhouse due to shit going on there. Which explained why Stoney and the rest of the guys didn't come down. I felt bad not having Stoney here, however, he called promising to check in with me to see how I was doing next time he came down. That doesn't mean he doesn't call me every day; you'd think the man is my father with as much as we talk. Hell, he might as well be, he's talked to me more than my own parents ever have. Shoot, my mom and dad don't even know I'm married.

As much as I've loved every minute with Rage, we've had our spats. For one, we got into it again over me working in the yard, though it wasn't exactly about the yard work more or less, but the fact I was using the weed eater barefoot with hardly any clothes on. Let's just say my ass ended up being a bright shade of red right there on the back porch where he spanked it then proceeded to fuck me against the rail. The good thing about having no neighbors, we can have sex outside.

Other than the few fights, everything else has been great. We even went not long ago and had Burner place another tattoo along my front. It wasn't easy due to the scarring, however, he did it. Blending them into the background of the design. He also put Rage's name within the tattoo. I never thought about getting a tattoo until Rage brought me to get the one on my back, now, I think I'm addicted and want to have both pieces attached somehow with the animals on my back swirling around to the front.

Something else has been happening in the last month. I have to figure out how to tell Rage about it. I'd started receiving strange messages, mostly harmless. Then the other day, I left work to run to get us some lunch, when I came back out of the restaurant, I noticed a piece of paper placed on my windshield. Opening it up, I didn't know what to think of the words, 'LEAVE OR ELSE'. What does it mean? I really should give it to Rage and tell him about the rest of the messages I have on my phone.

I'd placed the note in my purse, planning on telling him later when we got home and that's where it still sits along with the one from earlier today that was wedged in the frame of the front door. I'd quickly stuffed it in my purse without reading it. I'm surprised Rage didn't see it when he came home. He's been stressed, hell, all the guys from the club seem to be stressed out over something and none of them seem to be sharing. Any time I've asked what was going on, Rage shrugs it off claiming its club business. Ugh, I hate those words with a passion.

Now, here I am sitting at home alone due to Rage needing to be at the clubhouse for church. He'd wanted me to come with him, hang out in the main room while I waited for him. After seeing the note today, I didn't feel like going anywhere. Grabbing my purse, I pull out the previous one, holding it up to the one from today, my stomach flutters nervously as I read both notes. The first one I knew what it said by heart but the second, panic consumes me at the words, 'TRASH THAT'S ALL YOU ARE HE WILL BE RID OF YOU SOON ENOUGH AS YOU WILL BE BACK WHERE YOU BELONG'. Reading the words over and over, I don't understand them. Jake's dead and even in my shocked state of mind, I still remember him dying in front of me. Something about the words doesn't sit right with me. I really need to give these to Rage when he gets home.

I practically jump out of my skin when the doorbell rings. Who would be coming by here this late in the evening? Granted, it's almost Fall; the sun still hasn't set yet mostly due to the time change. Walking to the door, I'm shaking as I peek through the window next to it to see who it is. There's no one there, then I notice one of the floral companies' vehicles driving away though. Taking a breath, I open the door to find a bouquet of lavender flowers with a card attached.

Smiling, I bend over to pick up the vase, taking the card in hand as I stand back up. Walking back into the living room, I place the bouquet on the coffee table wanting to enjoy them. Sitting down, I open the envelope pulling the card out. My smile drops at the realization the flowers aren't from Rage but whoever it is stalking me. 'LEAVE BEFORE I MAKE YOU. DON'T MAKE ME BURY YOU SIX FEET UNDER BITCH.'

Unable to stop myself, I rush to the bathroom, barely making it to the toilet before all the contents in my stomach come out. Who'd go to such lengths to send flowers with this message attached to it?

Feeling dizzy, I sit back, drawing my knees up to my chest, letting the words on all three notes spin around in my head. Those notes have me seriously freaked to the point I don't want to be home alone right now. Standing up, I quickly glance in the mirror, seeing nothing other than pure terror in my own eyes. I don't have many choices on where to go right now considering during the week, everything, for the most part, closes early besides Outlaw Racks and the clubhouse.

Deciding it would be best to go straight over to the clubhouse, figuring I'd be able to show Rage the notes and tell him about the messages on my phone, I grab my keys and head out the door, making sure to lock it behind me. The last thing I need is for someone to waltz right in our house and invade my personal space. It's bad enough whoever this is knowing where I live.

Climbing in Rage's truck, I'm on the verge of a panic attack. I floor it, heading toward the clubhouse the moment I'm on the road. Needing the safety I only ever feel when I'm in his arms.

With the speed I'm running, I'm surprised I don't get pulled over, not even when I pass one of the unmarked police cars. Usually, they're biting at the bit to catch someone speeding and since I'd been hitting eighty ninety the whole way, I was for sure he'd clocked me.

Making it to the clubhouse in record time, I barely have the truck in park before storming inside, spotting a couple of prospects milling around the main room. If there was one outside, I didn't see them with my only focus on getting to Rage.

"You okay, Cleo?" Ace asks, coming around the bar.

"Ummm no, well I don't know. I need to see Rage," I murmur shaking my head barely able to breathe properly.

"They're all in church right now, babe. Why don't you sit down, I'll get you a water or something while you wait," Ace suggests, moving closer in my direction.

My body is visibly shaking when he goes to touch me. Screaming, I move away from him, taking off running through the clubhouse knowing exactly which room to run to. Normally, I'd never do this but, in my defense, I'm not thinking clearly. Rushing down the hall, I slam through the door to the room.

"What the fuck?" someone yells out. Several of the guys are standing, guns trained my way ready to shoot.

Oh, shit, maybe I shouldn't have barged in like this.

"Cleo, what the fuck?" Twister growls out

"Lave, baby, what are you doing here? And what are you thinking barging in here when you know we're having church?" Rage says, narrowing his eyes as he moves to stand directly in front of me.

"I . . . I . . . I'm so . . . sorry," stuttering, I begin to back away. "I'll go wait in the main room at the bar until you're done. Sorry guys," I murmur, turning to leave the room.

"Not so fast, baby," Rage catches my wrist, halting my leaving. "What's wrong? You'd never do this unless something was wrong."

"I needed you. I don't know how to explain this without you getting totally pissed with me but here it is." Pausing, I pull out the notes I'd thankfully put in my pocket before leaving the house. Considering I'd left my purse at home. Handing him the notes, he scans them, and I take a breath and begin. "A few weeks ago, I started to get these strange messages on my phone, then the other day, I received the first note on my car when I went to get lunch. Then another one today was wedged in the door frame at home. The last one from the floral company was attached to a thing of flowers that were left on the front porch a little while after you left. I thought they were from you at first and then I read the card, freaked, and here I am. I'm sorry I barged in here the way I did but I wanted to feel safe." My last words are barely more than a whisper as tears begin to sting my eyes.

Rage pulls me against him without saying a word. Even with the tension filling his body at everything I said, he gives me exactly what I need. His strength.

# CHAPTER TWENTY-ONE

## RAGE

Fuckin' hell, can this day get any worse? We'd been sitting here discussing the shitstorm beginning to boil around us when the door is slammed against the wall. Seeing my woman standing with panic pouring off her pisses me off. She's been through enough in her life to end with that look on her face. I don't even register my brothers putting their guns away. Everyone knows, including Cleo, that we're not to be bothered while in church unless it's an emergency. Then she hands me these papers. I'm scanning through them as she rambles on about what happened, my vision narrows.

Motherfucker, handing the notes to Gadget, I pull her into my arms, needing to hold her to me as much as I know she needs the same. I should be pissed at her for not telling me this shit before now and I'll be having words with her later on about it, however, right now's not the time or place.

I don't know who sent those notes or the flowers but I'm gonna find out one way or another. A couple of my brothers and I have to head out in a couple of days to receive a shipment, we'll be taking more brothers with us than normal. The

Dragons Fire MC has made it known they're lying in wait. We've seen them on the cameras Dragon, Gadget, and Hades hooked up down at the docks. We're at fuckin' war with the Dragons Fire MC, who the fuck knows what they're capable of. Those motherfuckers are dirty and aren't against using women if it works in their favor. Damn, their Prez Ratchet didn't even blink at using his own daughter to hurt to go against Izzy. The crazy bitch even tried shit with Lynsdey too.

Sitting back down, I pull Cleo down into my lap, soothing her as each of the brothers takes a look at the notes.

"Who the fuck would be after you, Cleo?" Horse asks gently.

"I . . . I . . . don't know," her voice is barely loud enough for anyone to hear besides me.

"Could it be Cristy doing this? Not to state the obvious but she has caused some trouble already," Twister throws out there, leaning forward, bracing his arms on the table.

"It's a possibility. She hasn't been seen since the party we threw for Rage and Cleo when they got married a few months back," Gadget speaks up, typing away on his laptop.

"Why would she want to do something like this?" Cleo gasps as she looks up from my chest.

"Baby, you can never underestimate a woman scorned. She was pissed when you put her in her place, could be looking for retribution," I tell her brushing a strained of hair from her face.

"Well, let's pause church for right now. Rage, why don't you take your woman home and take care of her. We'll reconvene tomorrow morning. See if we can find out anything about this and go over the details for the run coming up," Twister orders, banging the gavel down on the table causing Cleo to jump in my arms.

Her movement didn't go unnoticed. Lifting her up in my arms as I stand, I carry her out of the clubhouse, spotting my truck haphazardly parked in the lot. Walking toward it, I decided to leave my bike here for the night. I'll get it tomorrow, one way or another. I hate to have one of the guy's ride my bike to the house but if need be, I'll get Burner to do it for me. Not that I don't trust them with my bike, it's simply a sacred thing—no one drives my girl but me.

Pulling out of the parking lot, I keep her hand in mine, not wanting her out of my grasp for a minute, not knowing she's scared out of her mind. The words on those notes are burned into my brain. When I find whoever this sick fuck is I'll be sure to do what they threatened her with. I'll put them in the ground. No one, and I mean no one, will fuck with my woman.

Glancing over at Cleo in the dark of the night as I drive, I can make out her slumped form in the passenger seat. She's passed out. The stress of this bullshit must have been getting to her. Questions swarm my head, why didn't she come to me sooner? Did she not trust me to protect her from this shit? One thing I do know, come morning, she and I will be hashing this shit out. Tonight, though, I'm gonna hold her to me, not letting the demons take hold of her. I made peace with mine several years ago with what happened to Janie. It may still fuck with me from time to time, especially with the Diaz Cartel popping their heads back out of the sand, however, I don't have the nightmares like I used to.

Pulling into the driveway, I park the truck, turning off the engine quickly. I look around the dark, checking for anything out of place before getting out. Walking around the truck, I feel as if someone is watching us. Keeping my eyes on my surroundings, I pick Cleo up in my arms, holding her close to me as I make my way toward our house. Unlocking the door, I don't turn any lights on, heading straight for our room and placing her in the middle of the bed. Kissing her gently on the top of her head before leaving the room, needing to make sure the house is locked up tight for the night.

As I walk past the living room, I spot the flowers she told me about. Looking at them, I see right away why she'd think they were from me. It looks like a batch I'd get her. Purple is Cleo's favorite color, it's why she keeps her hair lavender. I smile as a memory hits me, the first time I spoke to her, I'd called her Lave and it stuck. She'd screwed up her face asking me why I kept calling her that. I'd simply lifted a hand to her hair and said, *'Your hair, babe, it's purple and you smell like lavender'.* The smile she'd given me was priceless. It was the beginning of the two of us and I'll be damned if someone is gonna fuck that up for the two of us now by taking something as special as purple flowers away from her. Those are for me to give her and no one else.

Picking the vase up, I go to the back door, unlocking it and head for the trash can. Dumping the vase, I turn on my heels and head back in, still feeling eyes on me. My gut is twisting, letting me know something isn't right. Reaching in my pocket, I pull out my phone and send a text to Ace, one of the prospects, ordering him and Shadow to be lookouts for the night. My head isn't on straight, otherwise, I'd be out hunting the tree line for whoever is out there. At his reply, I lock all the doors and head to bed. Maybe tomorrow after church, I'll talk to Gadget about a security system being put in here. Should've done it sooner.

Stripping out of my clothes, I climb into bed, pulling my woman against me. At the sound of her whimpering in her sleep, I run my hand through her hair soothingly until she calms back down.

Damn, tonight's gonna be a long as fuck night.

# CHAPTER
# TWENTY-TWO

## CLEO

*Laughter fills my ears as I look around the field full of lavender flowers. I smile, taking off running after the giggling little boy. "Momma, you can't get me," the little boy yells out over his shoulder.*

*"Oh, I'll catch you, you little booger." Laughing, I sprint to catch him right before he falls. "See, baby, I told you I'd catch you, I'll always catch you." I kiss his forehead. He looks so much like his daddy.*

*"I know you will, Mommy, and I'll always be right here in your heart. But Mommy, it's time to be all the way happy. I don't know what that means but be happy with Daddy. Take care of my baby sister and brothers, let them know I'm with them too," he whispers placing a hand on my cheek.*

*"Reagan, I could never forget you. You're my precious little boy, my little king," I say giving him an Eskimo kiss.*

*"I love you, Mommy. Will you tell Daddy I love him too for me?"*

*"Yeah baby, I'll tell him, he loves you so much."*

*"I know he does. I have to go now, Mommy, no more crying and remember, take care of my brothers and sister. They need you to be strong for them. Just like you were for me."*

*A single tear rolls down my cheek as he vanishes from my sight.*

Opening my eyes, I blink at the sunlight streaming into the bedroom. Peace falls over me as I vividly remember the words. Words of which I know my little boy will always be in my heart as well as Rage's. God, he would have been the most beautiful baby we could've asked for. Hair and eyes just like his daddy's with my dimples, the perfect combination. What did he mean though, take care of his baby sister and brothers? Does it mean I'm ready to talk to a doctor and see if, by a miracle, I can carry a child? Or if I'd need a surrogate. At which point, would I feel okay with someone else carrying my child, feeling everything I wanted to feel.

"What are you thinking so deeply about over there?" Rage whispers pulling me deeper into his embrace.

"About the dream I was just having," I murmur.

"Oh yeah, what was it about?"

"You're gonna think it's crazy."

"Babe, I don't think anything you could say would be crazy unless it was dancing monkeys and flying pigs," he says, giving me a squeeze.

Wanting to see his face as I tell him about our beautiful little boy in my dream, I turn in his arms. "Okay, so don't laugh but I had this most beautiful dream filled with the sweet sounds of a little boy's laughter," I start, keeping my gaze on his, seeing his eyes soften. I go on to tell him all about my dream. Of the little boy who looked so much like him with his eyes. And how he'd said to tell his daddy he loved him. Tears stream down my face as I finish by telling him he told me we needed to take care of his little sister and brothers. Eerie as it is, my dream seemed to ease some of the hurt and pain in my heart.

After what feels like hours of silence between us while Rage runs his fingers up and down my back gently, he finally breaks it. "That's a beautiful dream, Lave. There's nothing wrong with dreaming about our boy. He's a part of you and I both, and we'll never forget him. Why don't we pick a name for him and have Burner draw something up to honor him?"

"I'd like that," I whisper, running my fingers along his chest. "But I should tell you in my dream I called him Reagan."

"Reagan," he repeats smiling. "I love it, baby. It's perfect for him."

"Do you think you'd be okay with it if I made an appointment to find out what our options are for having kids?" I ask quietly.

"Lavender, baby, I love you and when you're ready to talk to a doctor, I'll be right there with you. Just remember one thing for me."

"What's that?"

"Whether it's meant to be or not, I'll always be right here," he says, placing his hand against my heart as he leans in gently kissing me.

"And the same with you, Travis, I love you so much," I murmur against his lips.

"I love you too, baby, but just so you know, after I fuck you like I want to, you and I are gonna have a word about you keeping shit from me," Rage says right before slamming his mouth onto mine and sliding his tongue inside, mingling with my own.

Wrapping my arms around his neck, I kiss him passionately. Rage pulls back long enough to rip my shirt over my head. Usually, I don't go to bed with anything on, liking the feel of his skin against mine. But I didn't get to remove them last night due to passing out in the truck on the way home.

Rage's mouth finds my lips once more, giving me a demanding kiss before moving down and kissing along my throat then down further, lifting my bra up over my breasts, taking a nipple into his mouth. Moaning, my back arches at the way he lavishes one nipple then the other.

"Fuck, Lave, I don't think I'll ever be able to get enough of these beauties," Rage says huskily as he moves further down my body, removing the rest of my clothes as he goes. Soon as he has my bottoms removed, he throws my legs over his shoulders and blows a breath against my pussy. I can't help but wiggle trying to get him to do more. I need more. His touch is mesmerizing.

Glancing down, I find him staring up my body. The moment our eyes meet, he latches onto my clit, sending bolts of lightning up my spine. Oh, shit, that's fuckin' unbelievable, the sensation is one I've never experienced in my life. Not even with him. He continues profusely attacking my clit while sliding a finger into my pussy, finding my spot, immediately sending me over the edge.

"Travis," I scream out coming harder than I could imagine. My body is still twitching as he kisses his way back up my body. Lining himself up, he barely thrust inside me, teasing me with the head of his dick. I groan when he pulls back.

"What do you need, baby?" he asks his voice strained.

"I need you inside me," I whimper as he repeats his motions repeatedly.

"I am inside you," he says.

"I mean all the way inside me. I need you all the way, Travis, please," I say close to begging. This is pure torture to have him tease with thrusting only the head in my pussy. It should be a crime.

"Are you going to keep shit hidden from me again?" His voice is firm.

"No, I didn't mean to. I'd planned to tell you last night when you got home," I cry out, frustrated he's using sex against me. Damn him!

"You should have told me the moment this shit started. I don't give a damn if it's a fuckin' paper cut you get. You tell me. No one fuckin' hurts you, ever. I told you, you're mine and I will always protect you," he says through clenched teeth right before plowing deep inside me. "Fuck, baby, you're nice and tight for me. Like always," he moans, thrusting in and out of me in controlled movements. "Damn beautiful seeing you this way, you light up like a fucking ball of fire for me."

Unable to think of a coherent thought, I reach for him, pulling him in, giving him a kiss I hope shows all I mean to say. Words and I have never mixed well together, showing him with my body is way easier. And that's what I do— kissing him deeply while running my fingers along his back, scratching him in the process.

It's like time stops and before I know it, I'm screaming out his name as I come, clenching his dick. He follows behind me seconds later, groaning, keeping his dick seated deep inside my pussy.

Putting his forehead against mine, Rage kisses me lightly before rolling to his side. It takes both of us several minutes to be able to calm our breathing down.

"Damn, baby, your pussy is gonna snap my dick in half one of these days with how tight it squeezes me," he says jokingly.

"Shut up about my pussy doing something like that," I giggle, slapping at his chest.

"It's the truth, woman, best damn pussy in the world," he grins gaining an eye roll from me.

"In all seriousness, Cleo, next time shit happens, whether it's big or small, you tell me immediately. Got me?" he orders.

"Yeah, Travis, I'll tell you. Does this mean you're not pissed at me?"

"Oh, I'm pissed, baby, but not at you. I'll admit I was last night but laying here last night holding you, I came to realize a few things, one being you didn't tell me at first because you thought I was too busy to deal with something like this. Which I'll tell you one more time to reiterate my point, when it comes to you, I'll jump through fire to do what I gotta do to keep you safe. Even if the club is dealing with shit."

"What is the club dealing with? And before you say club business, you know I'm not gonna say shit."

"Cleo, as much as I want to talk about this shit with you, I don't want you knowing unless I absolutely need to."

"Will you at least tell me something?" I push.

Sighing, he rolls to his back, taking me with him. "This is the only thing and I mean the only fuckin' thing I'm gonna tell you and I don't want you asking me questions about it," he says, his gaze serious. Nodding, I wait for him to tell me. "The Dragons Fire MC has started a war with us. They want to use the docks we use to transport their shit. We're not having it. We don't approve of what those fuckers do and before you ask, no I won't tell you what that is. Just know, we got this shit."

"Okay, thank you," I say leaning in and kissing him once more. "Now, how about we get up and I'll make us breakfast."

"Sounds good to me. Then I gotta get to the clubhouse and you're coming with me this time," he says, swatting my ass.

Squealing, I jump up off the bed, grabbing his shirt from yesterday and head to make us some breakfast to start the day.

# CHAPTER
# TWENTY-THREE

## RAGE

We finally make it to the clubhouse after I have Cleo again for breakfast, feasting on her with whipped cream, and damn if she wasn't delicious. Then taking her in the shower before we left the house. Watching her walk, I grin seeing her have the slightest waddle.

Needing to get to church, I sit her at the bar. "Alright, babe, gotta get to church. Stay in here and don't get into any trouble," I tell her leaning in and kissing her.

"Alright, I guess I'll pull up one of my books on my phone and read," she says, digging in her purse to get her phone.

I raise one of my brows. "You reading one of them trashy romance novels?" I ask, having read some of the shit she reads.

"I wouldn't say Elizabeth Knox writes trashy romance books," she says, placing her hand on her hip.

"Whatever you say, babe," I smirk, seeing the sass come out. Cleo can become defensive over the authors she reads. I learned firsthand when I commented on a scene I read over her shoulder in one book she'd been reading about some dick and dildo action going on.

"I mean, it's MC romance, for God's sake and they're completely the shit. I mean hello, how am I gonna learn how to be a full-blown biker chick if I don't read up on alpha dog MC guys and the women in these books," she throws at me.

"Alpha dog MC guys? Seriously, Lave, you think this of your man?" Laughing, I joke at her reasoning.

"No, I think of you as my hot ol' man, who gives me amazing, mind blowin' orgasms," she says, laughing.

"That sounds better, now, be good and don't go anywhere. Got me?"

"Promise. I don't have anywhere to be anyway," she says, leaning forward to kiss me. Needing more, I take her mouth with a demanding kiss. Pulling her closer, Cleo moans into my mouth when she feels what she does to me.

"Get a fuckin' room," Burner yells out from the hallway entrance.

"Fuck you, Burner," I throw back at him. "Alright, babe, be good," I kiss her once more before pulling away. Shaking my head when I look down seeing my dick pressed against my jeans. "Damn, babe, if only I had time to take you to my room and fuck you right now. Instead, I'm gonna have to deal with blue balls until I can get back in that tight pussy of yours," I mutter.

"I'll take good care of you later for dealing with blue balls," she promises as I turn to leave her in the main room as I head to church.

---

"Alright, brothers, let's finish what we started discussing yesterday. Then we'll discuss this other shitstorm happenin' around us," Twister says, banging the gavel on the table. "Gadget, you were saying something about Ratchet and the Diaz Cartel yesterday?"

"Yeah, so as I was saying, I've been keeping my eyes on the Dragons Fire MC, mainly Ratchet and his VP, along with Miguel Diaz from the cartel using a back door into their main computer systems which isn't hard to do because in all honesty, they're both dumb as fuck with this shit. How I wasn't able to find the shit with Izzy sooner kills me. But anyway, back to what I was saying, Miguel has asked Ratchet to take on a contract with them in finding women for the Diaz Cartel to sell. They're trying to grow their business again after the slaughter Rage and Burner did on them. I'm gonna go ahead and throw this out there, Miguel may end up attempting to get some retribution on you two. According to one message I've read, they talk about you two and Miguel not being happy he lost so many men. There's also talk of them wanting to take down the Alcazar Cartel. They end up going after them, we will be in an all-out war with not only another MC but with two cartels," Gadget informs all of us.

"This is a complete cluster fuck," Hades growls out. "What the fuck are we supposed to do? We got shipments coming in for orders the other charters need picked up. We don't have time for a four-sided war."

"What we should do is contact the Alcazar Cartel and show them proof of what's goin' on. Show them we're not in this bull-shit. They have their shit coming in from the gulf side of Flor-ida, it'd cost them too much to use our docks here and they have more sense than to fuck with the Russians over the docks we use," Dragon advises us and damn if he doesn't have a valid point.

"Dragons right," I state the obvious. "If we can get informa-tion to the head of the Alcazar Cartel, it might distract the Dragons Fire MC and Diaz Cartel for the time being while we keep an eye on all of them. Who knows, maybe they will take each other out?"

"What if they still come at us? We need a game plan for a shitstorm to hit us," Burner says, eyeing me.

"Whether it works or not, I'll go ahead and put this out there, I'm goin' hunting. That motherfucker went into hiding once and got away from Burner and I. Ain't happenin' again. Janie deserves to rest in peace and until that fucker is dead, it can't happen," I declare not voicing the rest of the plan forming in my head. I know my brothers would have my back anytime, but I intend to finish this the way we started it— with Burner watching my back as I go in and slice the motherfucker's throat and shove his dick through the opening.

Silence fills the room as my brothers take in my words.

"Rage, I know you want to finish what you started and I won't hold you back, neither will I hold Burner back. You're right, Janie deserves to rest in peace. But I'm tellin' you right fuckin' now, you two aren't goin' rogue this time. We will have your back," Twister says sternly, looking between Burner and myself.

Knowing better than to argue with him, I nod my head in agreement.

"Alright, so do we all agree on contacting the Alcazar Cartel in regards to what the fuck is going on here?" Twister asks the room.

Ayes fill the room.

"Good. Gadget, I want you to work your magic and find who we need to send this shit to or contact. Now, on to what the fuck happened yesterday; those notes Rage's ol' lady received can't go ignored."

Curses fill the room at the mention of the notes to Cleo.

"Not to intrude on Cleo's privacy, and I'll start this by saying I didn't look at the messages between you two or the ones with the other ol' ladies, which by the way, you four need to put a lockdown on what those women talk about. Seriously weird reading shit about y'alls dicks and how you use them. Especially Horse and his super sperm dick," Gadget says, causing everyone in the room to laugh, several of the guys throw jokes. Clearing his throat Gadget continues. "I found an unknown number with several messages, all the same saying she needed to leave town. One states everything was better without her. Then the last one she received states leave or else." Gadget stops speaking, brows furrowed "Fuck, Rage you're about to flip your shit but before I tell you all someone text Ace, tell him to take Cleo's phone from her. She just received another message."

"What the fuck?" I yell slamming out of my seat.

"Sit down, Rage," Twister orders.

"Fuck that, this is my goddamn woman were talking about, tell me what the hell was in this message," I growl pacing in place. Vision turning red, I'm on the edge of flipping hearing this shit.

"Brother, calm down," Twister orders as Ace knocks on the door right before entering the room and handing the phone over.

"I don't know why you need her phone but she told me to tell you it's cruel and mean with some other bullshit for interrupting her in the middle of one of the good parts and she is now not going to do as she promised," Ace smirks looking in my direction, relieving some of the tension filling my body.

"Thanks, man, tell her I'll get her phone back to her soon, 'til then, she can rethink that decision to renege on that promise," I grumble.

"I'll tell her," Ace chuckles, closing the door behind him.

Sitting back down, somewhat calmer knowing she didn't see the message, I look in Gadget's direction. "What did the message say?"

"One, it has a picture attached to it of you carrying her in your arms," he states pulling the image up on the big screen. I fuckin' knew someone had been out there. Motherfucker. "Here's the message that came with it." Gadget switches the image on the screen from the picture to the text. My vision narrows as I read what it says. 'DID YOU ENJOY THE FLOWERS? THEY'RE BEAUTIFUL AREN'T THEY? LEAVE BEFORE I PUT THE NEXT SET ON YOUR GRAVE. YOU DON'T BELONG HERE BITCH.'

"Who the fuckin' hell is this piece of shit?" Thorn mutters. He's been quiet for the most part other than agreeing to what needs to be done or not. Thorn's usually easy going, however, since the shit with Lynsdey then finding out the connection with Hades, he hasn't been the same. I need to remember to pull him aside later. With all the shit happenin' with the club, neither of us have had a lot of time to chill preferring to spend our free time with our women. Yeah, we've talked at parties and shit but not got to the heavy shit. He still hasn't told Hades about his connection to Lynsdey.

Shaking my head, I turn my focus back to the issue at hand.

"Gadget, can you trace who sent this?" I ask.

"Not that simple. It would be a lot easier if they called instead of texting, since they didn't, I'll have to work my magic and see if I can track it. I'll let you know what I find as soon as I do," he states eyes focused on his screen.

"Rage, Cleo needs to be put on lockdown. I don't care if she stays here or at y'alls house but until we know who's behind this, she shouldn't be left alone," Twister declares.

"Don't worry, Prez, Cleo isn't leaving my side other than when we have church. I'll let her keep her schedule the way it is and keep a prospect on her. We should put one on each of the women, make it seem like it's club business, so it doesn't draw attention to it being only her with protection," I suggest.

"Agreed. If nothing else for right now, let's get out of here and I'll message you all if something comes up between now and the next church meet," Twister says, banging the gavel down.

Standing up, I move toward my woman needing to put my

eyes her. She's my everything and I'll be damned if whoever this sick fuck is will get ahold of her.

They'll have to kill me first.

# CHAPTER
# TWENTY-FOUR

## CLEO

I can't believe Rage told Ace to take my phone from me. I mean seriously, I'd been right in the middle of a good part of the book. The suspense is killing me and I'm sitting here fuming at not being able to finish the chapter. You can say I become violent when someone messes with my books. I remember the first time Rage snatched a book out of my hand causing me to lose my page. I'd been so infuriated with him, I informed him he wouldn't get any sex from me that day. Did my threat work? No, it didn't. He ended up teaching me I couldn't use my body against him. However, Rage knew exactly how to use mine against me.

"He better have a good reason for taking my phone," I muttered to myself. Since I don't have my phone now, I might as well figure something else to do. I don't know how long they'll be, and I hate sitting around doing nothing.

Guess I could practice my aim on the pool table. No one's here to make crackpot jokes about me sending the cue ball off the side. As I move toward one of the tables, Ace comes back into the room smirking, "Rage told me to inform you to think on your decision to renege on your promise." Laughing, the asshole goes back to stocking the bar.

"Asshole," I mutter under my breath. Damn him if he thinks he's getting any right now.

Once I have all the balls racked up, I grab a pool stick off the wall, finding one that feels right in my hands. Rage has been helplessly trying to teach me and I admit, I suck ass. Lining the cue ball where I want it, I bend to take my first shot, missing the entire grouping. Damn. Looking up to make sure no one saw just how badly I am, I reach for the cue ball again doing the same thing. Though this time, I make contact, barely, but it's a start.

By the time I feel hands sliding over my ass, I'm more comfortable with myself having made several shots in a row. Might have been both stripes and solids but, hey, beggars can't be choosers. Standing up straight, I lean into the solid mass of chest standing directly behind me.

"You took my phone," I say accusingly.

"Yea, I did. I'll give it back later. You were doing pretty good over here, how many times you knock the cue ball off the table this time?" he asks with a shit-eating grin on his face. I'm sure my face is redder than a crayon at his question. Once, I knocked the cue ball off the table so hard it hit a clubwhore in the ass. Why did it hit her in the ass? The bitch had been kneeling, sucking Hades' dick. Talk about ewww. I usually don't pay attention to what the clubwhores do around here. Long as they leave Rage alone, I don't have a problem with them. They saw what I'm capable of when I beat Cristy up in front of everyone.

Shaking the memory off, I turn to face Rage. "I may or may not have knocked it off the table a few times but only when I started playing," I grumble. Still holding the pool stick in my hand, I touch his nose with the tip, leaving a dot of chalk behind.

"Well, you wanna finish this game by yourself or maybe

rack 'em and show me what you got?" he asks leaning down and kissing me quickly.

"We could play a game together. I've been practicing," I say smiling at him.

"I can see that." He grins though it doesn't quite reach his eyes. I tilt my head, getting a good look at Rage's expression. I know him well enough to know something is bothering him. Maybe a game of pool will help him relax some.

"We can even have a few beers if you want," I say while turning to rack the balls up for us.

"Sounds good, baby. How about for dinner tonight we do Chinese or something?" Rage asks moving to get his own pool stick.

"Whatever you want, Travis," I whisper when I'm standing right in front of him. Lifting a hand, I run it up his chest and curve it around his neck, pulling him down to my lips. "Just know, you're not off the hook for taking my phone, especially when I was at a really good part." Nipping at his lip, I pull out of his reach, grinning.

Seeing the heat in his eyes, I smile more.

"Challenge accepted, babe," Rage growls. Stepping forward, he reaches out and grabs me by my waist with one hand while throwing his pool stick down with the other. "You wanna renege on that promise of getting rid of my blue balls, you'll be playing with fire. Remember, Lave, I can make you hot and leave you wanting while I jack my dick off, spray it on your stomach, then go to bed later," he states right before slamming his lips down on mine.

Moaning, I drape both my arms around his neck, pulling myself against his body. Rage cups my ass and lifts me, so I have no choice but to wrap my legs around him.

Ending the kiss, I'm breathless. I put my forehead to his. "Maybe we can go home instead of staying for a game of pool," I sigh.

"Damn good idea, I need to be inside you fuckin' soon."

Giving me a devilish smile, he heads toward the main door, not bothering to put me down— not even when he reaches into his pocket to pull out the truck keys. "Ace, bring my truck to the house later today and don't fuck with her. I find a scratch anywhere on my paint job, I'll beat the shit out of you," he yells tossing the keys to Ace.

"That's not very nice, Rage," I say.

"Lave, baby, there's three things you don't fuck with when it comes to me. You don't fuck with my woman ever. My bike is right up there with you, followed closely by my truck." The serious look Rage gives me makes me want to laugh but I don't.

"Well then, at least I'm first on that list. How about you take me home and show me exactly how correct that statement is?" Leaning forward, I kiss his neck.

# CHAPTER
# TWENTY-FIVE

## CLEO

My hands are shaking as I sit here waiting on test results. Rage sits beside me, running a hand down my back supportively. Over the past three weeks, several things have happened. Some scary and some pretty amazing.

First thing had been Rage informing me I'd have a prospect on me for the time being due to the threat I'm facing. He also informed me of the reason Ace took my phone when he did—then proceeded to lecture me on discussing dick sizes with the girls. I simply told him I didn't need to compare notes on who has the best dick. Damn Gadget for reading our group chat. Kenny, Izzy, and Lynsdey agree with me that when it's time to get our revenge on him, it's gonna be great. We all know him and Dragon have the hots for Dr. Connors.

Next thing to happen is Izzy and the rest of us started putting the final touches on the Letters from Above charity event. They even convinced me to sing on stage with Chaz, the lead singer of Demons Among Us. Chaz refused to let the subject drop having heard me sing on occasion. Talk about wanting to pee my pants thinking of singing in front of hundreds of people. Rage wasn't too fond of the idea at first, then he'd come to pick me up the other day and heard me singing on the stage while Chaz played his guitar. My eyes locked on his and I sang Jo Dee Messina 'Bring on the Rain' right to him. That night when we got home, he rocked both our worlds and said I could sing to my heart's content.

And last, but not least, we made an appointment with a specialist, figuring it'd take weeks to get to see the doctor. However, they ended up having an opening the day we called. After speaking to the doctor, they explained a few tests I'd have to do in order to see if I'd be able to have another baby. They'd also need to do an ultrasound of my uterus to see the damage done to it.

Now, here we are, sitting and waiting impatiently to find out the results from the test we had done.

"Baby, calm down. Whatever Dr. Longsten says, we'll be okay. Remember, we have options," Rage says, pulling me out of my head.

"I know, I guess I'm really nervous. Have been since doing these test a week ago. You know how difficult it is to focus on things when something this important hangs out in the air? It's not easy, that's for sure," I ramble on ready to get this over with. I've dreaded getting my hopes up for any type of miracle but I'm anxious to see what the doctor has to say.

"It's gonna be fine, Lavender, just fine," he states, kissing my forehead.

"Thank you, Travis," I sigh, taking in his strength.

A knock at the door has me sitting back up straight. "Good morning, Cleo, Rage, how are you two?" Dr. Longsten asks as she walks into the room. I'd been apprehensive about any doctor besides Dr. Connors due to all the shit that's gone on but Connors recommended her. And I couldn't be more thankful to have listened. From the moment I first met Dr. Longsten, she has been nothing but supportive, answering every question we have. I guess it comes with practice.

"Hey, Dr. Longsten, we're both doing good. I guess you could say I'm anxious to see what the results are."

"Well, let's get rid of that anxious feeling you're having now. I've got your results right here. Now, I am somewhat concerned about the scarring to your uterus and it may become an issue later in the pregnancy where you'll have to go on bed rest as to not strain your body. Oops, sorry, I have a habit of jumping right in. Let me rewind really quick. Congratulations, you two are having a baby according to your test results," she says, smiling.

Words escape me as I take in the news. Stunned, I turn to look at Rage. He has the biggest smile on his face as he stares at me. "We're gonna have a baby, Lave," he says, cupping my cheek.

"Yes, now I'd like to do another ultrasound to see if we can get a look at the little nugget. Also due to the scarring, I'll be classifying your pregnancy as high risk. You will have to come into the office more often in order to make sure you and the baby are both progressing properly."

"Okay," I whisper, my mind whirling a mile a minute, thinking back to that dream I had of Reagan. I look down at the inside of my wrist, seeing the precious tattoo I had put there by Burner. Yea that was one other thing Rage and I did during the past few weeks. He'd taken me a couple of days after my dream to have this tattoo done. He'd gotten the same one, though his sits right under his collarbone. Burner free-handed a heartbeat with our baby's name scrolled through the lines.

"If you have any questions or think of any before your next appointment, please feel free to contact me. Now, let's get you down the hall to the ultrasound room. I'm gonna personally do the ultrasound today to see where we're at," Dr. Longsten says, guiding the two of out of the room.

My mind is having a hard time comprehending the fact I'm pregnant. She must be wrong. There's no way. The other doctor told me I wouldn't be able to carry a child.

"Alright, Cleo, I want you to remove your pants and underwear while I step out of the room for a moment. Use this to cover your lower half," she says, handing me the sheet from the cabinet.

"Okay," I say again unable to speak otherwise. I can hear my heart racing in my ears.

"Lavender, you okay, baby?" Rage asks, standing in front of me.

"Um, I don't know," I tell him honestly.

"Well, let's get through this next part, maybe then you'll feel better," he says, softly placing a kiss to my forehead.

Nodding, I quickly strip out of my jeans, pulling my underwear down with them. Bending over, I pick them up to fold them before placing them on the chair next to the exam table.

Rage quietly lifts me off the floor, placing me on the exam table. The crinkling sound of the paper is the only noises to be heard in the room. Unfolding the sheet, I place it over my lap and wait for Dr. Longsten to come back in. Thankfully, we don't have to wait for very long. She comes back in smiling sweetly at the both of us.

"Okay, Cleo, I want you to lie back and put your feet in the stirrups. I'm going to be doing a vaginal ultrasound today. The next time, we'll be doing it over your stomach. However, I don't believe you're far enough along to be able to see anything that way."

I nod my head in agreement, waiting for her to get setup. When she's ready, she grabs a remote, turning a large TV screen on behind her. Furrowing my brow, I stare at the TV wondering why she turned it on.

I feel her insert the wand inside me, not once taking my eyes off the screen in front of me. Then I see it and my eyes widen. Holy shit, my heart skips a beat, Dr. Longsten wasn't wrong.

"And there he or she is." Her words draw me out of my trace. "It looks as if you are seven weeks and three days along," she says all the while doing measurements.

Turning my head, tears fill my eyes as I find Rage sitting next to me, his eyes on the screen. He looks mesmerized by the small peanut. He must feel me staring at him because he turns his gaze to meet mine and the smile he graces me with sends any lasting worries out of my head.

"I love you, Lavender. I can't tell you how fuckin' much I love you but I do," his voice fills with emotion. Rage stands, moving to stand by my head. Cupping my cheek with one hand, he places his other on my stomach. Leaning in, he kisses me, right then and there, not caring the doctor is still in the room with us.

"I love you," I tell him, blushing at the smile on Dr. Longsten's face. I hadn't even noticed she'd removed the wand and was now removing the gloves from her hands.

"Alright, Cleo, these are for you." She hands me the pictures of our little baby. "I want to see you back here in two weeks instead of four. I want you to take it easy. As I stated earlier, you will be classified as a high risk due to the severity of the scars. I will, if I deem it necessary, put you on bed rest at any point I feel that's what needs to happen. Now, why don't you get dressed and I'll leave a packet of information for you at the front desk for you to pick up. Congratulations again. I'm happy to see we weren't gonna have to go the long way around giving you both this miracle," she says, moving toward the door.

I slide off the table the moment the door is closed, handing the images to Rage. I quickly get back into my clothes, my mind reeling with excitement. Holding these pictures make everything seem more than real.

This time will be different. This time, I will do anything to protect our child. Even if it means lying in bed twenty-four seven.

"Come on, baby, let's get out of here, I wanna show you just how happy I am," Rage says, taking hold of my hand and pulling me into his side as we make our way out of the room.

"Okay, can we get Chinese on the way home?" I ask, smiling.

"You can have whatever the fuck you want, baby," he murmurs against my forehead.

"Well, in that case, I want to go pick up some lo mein noodles and then binge-watch Criminal Minds on Netflix." I giggle when he narrows his eyes at the mention of Criminal Minds. I'd recently started watching it and have become obsessed with the different crimes the team profiles. I especially like watching Shemar Moore.

"Then let's get home," he says.

Smiling, I go to make my next appointment.

# CHAPTER
# TWENTY-SIX

## RAGE

My mind is still reeling even days later after Cleo and I found out she's pregnant. As much as I'm fuckin' thrilled to be a dad and watch my woman grow round with my child, I'm nervous as hell with all the shit still up in the air trying to find whoever it is stalking Cleo on top of this silent war. Thankfully, it's been at a standstill with the Dragons Fire MC, though I don't know how long that will last.

The Alcazar Cartel responded, thanking us for informing them of the matter between Dragons Fire and the Diaz Cartel. The leader of the Alcazar Cartel personally came up here and met not only Twister but Stoney and Hammer as well. According to Twister, he'd come personally to show no ill will against us. And that if it comes to a war with the Diaz Cartel and Dragons Fire MC, they would not put us in the middle. It doesn't mean we will be kept from the war; we all know those fuckers are aiming for our territory along with the docks.

Grigory, our contact for the Russians, has even stepped in stating if those fuckers want a fuckin' war, he has no problem pulling his blades back out. Fuckin' crazy as shit when he'd come to the clubhouse. I thought my mouth would have fallen to the ground eyeing his bike. I'd met him several times down at the dock where we'd meet up to accept the shipment. When he first took over for the other guy, I found it weird he showed up at each shipment delivery. "No one fucks with the shipment on my watch," he'd told Thorn and I that first time. Now, I'm used to seeing the man anytime we go to the docks, however, this was the first time he'd come to the clubhouse to let us know he had no problem backing us if need be.

The charity event Izzy has been planning for months is coming up soon and we've all been helping get shit set up. Cleo is a nervous wreck about singing on stage. I know at first I'd been against it but didn't say no, though, I'd change my mind the moment I heard her on stage singing a song that I've never heard before. My heart clenched at the lyrics. The best part, she'd kept her eyes on me from the moment I walked in.

We still haven't told anyone about the baby. She wants to be out of the first trimester before, as she puts it, she spills the beans. I don't blame her for wanting to keep this to ourselves. We might not have known about her being pregnant with Reagan but knowing we lost our first child makes it where we merely want to savior the news. At least for a few more weeks. Cleo's been researching everything under the sun regarding what she can do and what not. Nervous about being sure to not lose our baby. I'm pretty sure until our baby is born, she's gonna freak at every little thing.

My phone ringing draws my attention back to the present. I put the wrench I'm using down to grab my phone. Glancing at the screen my brows furrow, UNKNOWN.

"Yeah," I ask answering the phone curious as to who would call me from an unknown number. Especially after I had Gadget work his magic and set it up where any unknown numbers should be blocked completely from mine and Cleo's phone.

Heavy breathing fills the line right before they disconnect.

Fucking weird as shit, I think to myself. Soon as I put my phone down, it rings again. What the fuck?

Picking it back up, I answer the call, "What the fuck do you want?" I growl, not wanting to play these phone games.

The same heavy breathing fills the line.

"Look, motherfucker, I don't know who the fuck you are but I ain't got time for this bullshit." Growling, I move toward the open bay of the garage. My gut is telling me this is Cleo's stalker and I damn sure don't need her hearing this shit if she wanders out of the office.

The heavy breathing turns into a distorted laugh. "You think you can protect her from me. There's nowhere that bitch can hide. Since she won't leave, I have no choice but to kill her. She took everything from me, everything that I wanted and now it's time for her to pay what's due. You will not be able to keep her from me," the voice on the other end of the line proclaims.

*Motherfucker!*

Taking the phone from my ear, I shoot Gadget a text to see if he can track the call. Placing the phone in my pocket, I head back inside making my way to the office. Without setting my eyes on Cleo to make sure she's okay, I won't be able to get shit done.

Soon as I walk into the office, Cleo looks up from the computer and gives me a smile. "You know the baby is the size of a raspberry right now," she says, placing her hand on her belly. And just like that, she has me smiling. Fury still burns through me knowing the threat coming toward us, however, her simple statement brings a smile to my face.

"Is that right?" I ask her, moving around the desk. Kneeling next to her, I turn the chair she's sitting in. Lifting her shirt, I place a kiss to her belly. "Hey, my little peanut, your daddy loves you," I murmur where our baby grows. I can't fuckin' wait to see her stomach round.

"Did you need me to do anything?" Cleo asks running a

hand through my hair. Closing my eyes, I soak in her tenderness.

"Naw, babe, I just wanted to make sure you were doing okay in here," I say giving her a reassuring smile.

"Oh, okay. Can we head home soon? I want to get dinner started," she asks.

"Fine with me, I'm done for the day. Let's head out," I tell her, holding my hand out to help her up. She might not be showing yet but the need to help her do anything, even stand, overpowers everything else.

"Great, I'm ready to get into comfy clothes too," she mumbles as she takes my hand.

"Lavender, you know you can wear whatever the fuck you want here?" I say gently.

"I know but I don't want to seem unprofessional when I speak to a customer." I get where she's coming from. She wants to do right by her job here at the garage but none of us would give a damn if she came to work in sweats and a hoodie. Long as the work got done.

Making sure the office is locked for the day, I shout over to Hades, letting him know we're heading out. At his nod, I guide Cleo out to the truck.

At the feel of my phone going off, I pull it out to find Gadget responded to my text. Opening it up while I round the front of the truck, I'm pissed to find out the number he traced was a burner. I fucking should've realized this, damnit.

I don't bother texting him back. Instead, I shove my phone in my pocket. Nothing can be done about this tonight. I'll text Twister when we get home as well as make sure the prospects are guarding the house tonight.

I'll be damned if this asshole gets anywhere near my woman.

# CHAPTER
# TWENTY-SEVEN

## CLEO

Since finding out about the baby, I have been doing my research, needing to be sure I don't do anything to hurt our baby. At the garage earlier when Rage walked it the office, I knew he was pissed. The way he's demeanor changed, I knew something was wrong. Anger rolled off of him, and I figured it was time to go.

I can't say going home was a good idea. I'd been ready to get back into comfy clothes all day. This morning when I woke up, this nausea hit me full force. Granted, I didn't puke but the feeling stayed with me throughout the day. I know I'd told Rage I'd needed to get dinner started, however, all I want to do is take a nap. I'm exhausted.

Looking into the refrigerator, I'm trying to decide between stuffed pork chops or chicken and rice. Neither really sounds appetizing right now but we both need to eat. The feel of Rage wrapping his arms around me causes me to jump. I didn't hear him come up behind me.

"What's for dinner, baby?" Rage murmurs against my ear.

"I'm debating," I tell him.

"Debating? You never fucking debate on what to fix, babe." Chuckling, he moves me out of the way. I stare daggers into his back as he reaches inside, pulling out the chicken. "How about I throw these on the grill?" he suggests. God, I love this man.

"Sounds good to me. I'll make a salad and baked potatoes to go with them," I tell him moving back to the refrigerator to pull everything out to make the salad.

"Works for me, Lavender." Kissing me, he turns to head outside.

I don't know what happened at the garage, but he doesn't seem to be allowing it to affect him now. Maybe after dinner, I can get him to open up and let me know what's going on. I hadn't received any more messages from whoever it was sending them, not since the flowers were sent here to the house. Maybe whoever decided to stop. It might merely be wishful thinking, still, a girl can only hope. Right?

---

"Do you want to tell me what's going on?" I quietly ask Rage while the two of us snuggle in the bed. After dinner, he'd helped me clean up the kitchen then brought me up to the room where we explored every inch of each other's bodies.

"I don't know if I wanna tell you this shit, babe," he sighs running a hand along my back.

"What don't you wanna tell me?" My voice firm as I ask him. If it's something to do with me, I have the right to know. I refuse to be left in the dark.

Sighing, Rage moves to sit up, putting his back against the headboard. Pulling the sheet around me, I sit up to face him. "I'm only gonna tell you this since I know if I don't, you'll be pissed. That being said, remember, I will protect you no matter what. You understand?" At my nod, he tells me about the calls he received at the garaged. I begin to shake as panic starts to set in. I jump off the bed, running for the bathroom and making it to the toilet right when everything I'd had for dinner comes up. Oh, fuck! Who is doing this to me? Why? What do they mean I took everything from them? Question after question circulates in my head that I wish I had the answers to.

"I got you, baby," Rage says softly while pulling my hair back from my face. "I swear, Lavender, this sick fuck isn't gonna get to you or our baby. I can promise you that. I'll put a bullet through their skull first," his voice is firm but gentle as he tries to calm me down.

"I believe you, Travis, I do," I murmur ,sitting up. Rage pulls me into his embrace, giving me the support, I need.

"I love you," he whispers, placing a kiss on the top of my head. "Let's get you cleaned up and to bed." He stands, pulling me with him. At the sink, he lets me go long enough to brush my teeth and clean my face. *Ugh, puking.*

Once we're back in bed, we lay with my back flush against his chest, his arm wrapped around me lying protectively on my stomach. "We're gonna get through this," he says right before I fall asleep.

---

"Baby, I need you to wake up." Rage's voice breaks through the deep sleep I've been in. Grumbling, I roll over going back to sleep. "Lave, come on, you gotta get up. I need to get to the clubhouse. You can go back to sleep there."

"What time is it?" I ask sleepily.

"It's four-thirty, come on, we gotta get moving," he says, handing me some clothes.

Sitting up, I grab the first piece. "There better be a damn good reason for me to get up this earlier, especially when I can't have coffee," I mutter, sitting up to put my clothes on.

"You can go back to bed in our room there," he states, handing over my shoes once I'm dressed. I'm not even out of bed by the time Rage grabs my hand, pulling me with him through the house.

"Are you gonna tell me why we're heading to the clubhouse?" I grumble, getting in the truck.

"Emergency church, babe, can't say anything else right now," he says, starting the truck and pulling out of the driveway.

"Fine, you better be getting me some donuts later for this," I mumble staring out the windshield, seeing nothing but darkness ahead of me.

By the time we get to the clubhouse, a wave of nausea hits me and I barely get the door open before I'm puking right there in the lot. Damnit, this sucks. I hate this part. Other than last night, Rage didn't know I'd been dealing with nausea over the past couple of days. From what I'd read online, morning sickness usually started around eight weeks.

"You okay, baby?" he asks standing next to the truck. I'd still been sitting, hovering my head out the door.

"Yeah, I'm okay, just a spell," I say sitting back up to unbuckle my seat belt.

Sliding out of the truck, I avoid the spot on the ground where the contents from my stomach landed.

I glance up at Rage, his eyebrows furrowed.

"I'm okay, I swear, it's morning sickness," I assure him.

"This the first time?" he asks.

"No," I whisper embarrassed.

"Gotta tell me this stuff, Lave, I wanna be there for you. Got me?" he grumbles, pulling me against him. At my nod, he moves us toward the door. "Let me get you settled in the room then I gotta get to church."

"Okay," I say more than happy to lay back down. I could use a few more hours of sleep.

Once in the room, Rage makes sure I'm good before leaving. The moment my head hits the pillow, I fall right back to sleep. Not wanting to spare a thought to what emergency church is for right now. I know I will later though.

# CHAPTER TWENTY-EIGHT

## RAGE

When my phone rang this morning, I didn't answer it the first time. Then it rang again and I knew it was important. No one in their right fucking mind would call me at this time of morning. I didn't want to wake Cleo up; she'd been sleeping peacefully.

Once I have her settled in our room, I make my way back into the main room to grab a cup of coffee. I'm gonna need it. I find several of my brothers doing the same thing. No one speaks as they pour themselves a cup. I spot Izzy behind the bar grabbing more cups for everyone.

"Sweetheart, go back to bed. These fuckers can get their own coffee mugs," Twister says, moving closer to her and placing a hand protectively on her belly. I can't help smiling even at this ungodly hour at the two of them. Both of them deserve to be happy.

"Well, I'd still be asleep right now if this child weren't kicking me every two seconds," Izzy states, turning her head to look at her ol' man. Watching the two of them is hilarious as fuck. I couldn't ask for a better ol' lady for our Prez. She might have been through hell but she's one strong ass woman.

"Izzy, you should listen to your ol' man," I say gaining a huff from her. I smile as I lean over the top of the bar grabbing one of the mugs behind her. I have my own mug I use when staying here at the clubhouse. It even has my name on it, so no one fucks with it.

Pouring my coffee, I down half of it quickly, needing the brew to get in my system. Topping my cup off, I head toward the room we hold church in with the rest of my brothers. Twister comes in a moment later with a grim look on his face.

"Sorry to have to call you all in at this fucking hour. Shit's escalated early this morning brothers," Twister says the moment he takes his seat. "Got a call from Javier, head of the Alcazar Cartel. He reported someone attempted to take him out last night. We can only assume it was either the Diaz Cartel or the Dragons Fire MC. They've finally made the first move," he finishes slamming his fist down on the table.

"Did whoever do this leave a message behind?" Thorn asks.

"No, Javier said someone shot out the windshield of his car along with his tires," Twister's response has me sitting up straight. My gut tightens. I can take a guess at who it could've been. When Miguel went underground with only a hand full of his men left, one of them being Marco, his right-hand man and deadly with a sniper rifle. No way would the Dragons Fire MC have enough reach to get to Javier.

"What should we do?" Hades speaks up. "We have a run we're leaving for later today. Do we still go or hold off?"

"If we hold off, it puts us behind," Horse states and I know he's right.

"We continue with the run, everything's set up, nonetheless, so we take caution." My voice is stern as I speak up. I handle all the navigations of making sure we take the roads most secure. I know without a doubt we take the right ones, we can pick up the shipment and get back here safely.

"And what if we get ambushed while at the docks?" Burner asks.

"We'll take more men with us, leaving only a handful behind to watch the women," Twister announces. Usually, he and Horse stay behind, letting Thorn and I handle the shipments. If he's coming, I'm guessing he's got the same feeling I do— somethings up.

"I'll stay behind, Prez," Gadget speaks up without hesitation.

"Alright, then we'll head out in about two hours then. That gives us time to bring the rest of the women here and the kids," Twister says.

"I have something I need to tell y'all before we head out. Yesterday at the garage, I got a phone call from Cleo's stalker. I called Gadget right after, however, we weren't able to track the number. The voice was distorted to the point I couldn't tell if it belonged to a man or woman." Taking a breath, I go on to tell them the exact words the person said. Repeating the words angers me as if I just heard them.

"I'll be sure to keep her inside the clubhouse," Gadget says.

"Thanks, brother, I don't want anything happenin' to her or our baby," I say without thought to the last words. Fuck, I didn't mean to tell them about the baby, but I know without a doubt, they won't run their mouths.

"You tellin' us Cleo's pregnant?" Twister says, grinning.

"Yeah, she is. We found out a few days ago," I grin proudly. I don't need to tell them the struggles we thought we were facing.

"What the hells goin' on with this club?" Hades laughs. "I'm gonna have to stay away from the women here or keep them from drinkin' the water."

"Congrats, man," Thorn says, slapping my back, beginning the rounds or cheers as each of the brothers has something to say.

"Thanks, brothers, we weren't expecting to tell anyone for a few weeks so, keep it to yourselves," I tell them.

"You got it, Rage. Now, Gadget is staying behind, so be sure to not let any of the women out of the clubhouse. Station a prospect at each door, we don't want a repeat with what happened to Izzy," Twister says, eyeing Gadget.

"No problem there. I'll station myself in the main room with all my equipment to watch the security systems both here and at the docks," Gadget says assuredly.

"Good, now let's get out of here and get ready to go. Prep to be ready for anything. We don't know if anything will happen or not but, in my eyes, it can't be a coincidence for Javier to be attacked at the same time as us having a run," Twister says, slamming the gavel down, adjourning for now.

In two hours, we could be facing life or death. All I gotta say is if they ambush us, it'll be their deaths coming for them. Stepping out of the room, I head to my room wanting to spend a little more time holdin' my woman close.

---

Pulling up to the docks, we're definitely ahead of schedule. Leaving Cleo had been hard. I didn't wake her up when I took off. I did leave her a note though letting her know I'd be back later. The ride here was uneventful though right now, my gut is telling me things aren't right. Moving toward the cargo hold, no one is around.

I hold my hand up, signaling the guys behind me to stay put. I may be the Road Captain, and this is Hades' job being the Enforcer, but military experience is telling me to hold back.

"Someone's up ahead," I whisper not wanting my voice to carry any further than to my brothers.

"Thorn, you go around the other way to see if you can scope anything out," Twister orders.

Thorn takes off, leaving quietly. When he's out of sight, I

signal without words for Hades and Burner to follow me, leaving the rest of the guys to stay behind.

The first ping of a bullet hitting the cargo container is just the start. Dashing through the rows, I feel the sting of a bullet hitting my arm and another in my leg. Fuck that hurts. Rushing through, scanning the area, I spot the fucker who aiming at us. Well, at least one of them. I don't know how many are out there. Aiming the gun in my hand, I hit the dumbass square in the chest, sending him to the ground with one bullet.

"Brother, I don't know how many are out there, we gotta fall back," Burner suggest.

"Fuck that, I'm gonna finish this shit right here," I growl, moving forward and scoping out the area as I keep walking. Spotting Thorn, he signals how many he's seen so far. At least five more of these motherfuckers around. Nodding my head, I relay the information to Hades and Burner.

"You alright, Rage?" Twister asks catching up to us.

"Yeah, Prez, I'm good. We got at least five of these douchebags we need to take out," I say.

"Let's split up into three's and find them," Hades growls. Why he would suggest three, I'll never know.

Nodding my head, I move forward, figuring whoever is coming with me will catch up.

Finally, I spot two of them with Dragons Fire MC cuts on. Dumb fuckers need a lesson is staying out of our territory for the last time. Turning to glance behind me, finding both Hades and Burner, I lift a brow gaining a nod from each of them at my silent question. I turn my head back around, lifting my gun. Finding my target, I hit one as another bullet hits his buddy. Two down, three to go. The sound of a gun going off somewhere else signals another one going down, meaning we have two more left.

Moving forward, Burner and Hades right behind me, it doesn't take us long to find one of the last two considering he runs right toward us. His eyes widen as he skids to a stop the second he realizes his life's about to end.

The dumb ass lifts his gun, pulling the trigger at the same time I pulled my own. A burning in my shoulder has me dropping my gun. Motherfucker got me. Damnit, Cleo's gonna kill me for taken' three bullets today.

Thankfully, two of them are grazes, the one in my shoulder is not. It's lodged in there. Grimacing, I lean against the container behind me, the blood loss beginning to get to me. Looking down, I find my shirt is covered in blood.

"Rage, you good man?" Hades asks, pulling out a knife and ripping into my shirt with it. Once he has the shirt split in half, Burner helps with removing it, only to ball it up to press against the wound.

"We're gonna have to get you to a hospital, brother," Burner states.

"Fuck if I'm going anywhere but back to the clubhouse. I'm not gonna die. Dragon can take the damn bullet out there," I wince at the pressure he applies to my shoulder.

"Fine, but you can't ride, asshole," he grunts. Movement to the right catches my eye. Grigory.

"I miss the party already?" he asks, coming to stand by us.

The rest of the club members soon find us, dragging the asshole with them. "We need to get back to the clubhouse," Twister says, eyeing my shoulder.

"We can't leave the shipment behind," I tell him.

"You're right, we're not. Half of us will stay behind to load it up. Grigory, hate to ask but would your men be willing to help?" Twister turns to ask Grigory. Studying him, you can feel the darkness pouring off of him. No wonder he used to be the personal torpedo for the head of the Russians and known as the boogeyman. He's as deadly as they come.

"Yeah, Twister, they can do that. I'll even follow to be sure nothing else happens. These fuckers fucked themselves this time. No one fucks with the Russians," he starts spewing words in Russian none of us understand.

"Thanks, man. The club will owe you one," Twister says, holding his hand out to Grigory.

"I'll let you know if I'm ever in need of the club," Grigory states, taking Twisters hand.

"Well then, if alls good, can y'all get me the fuck out of here," I grumble, ready to get home to my woman.

"Yeah. Rage, Burner, Hades, and Dragon, you all head out with him and get his ass patched up. When the rest of us get back, we'll have church," Twister informs us.

Nodding my head, I move to stand up straight. Even with my knees weak, I refuse to lean on anyone as I move toward my bike. I don't give a damn if I'm bleeding out, I'll be riding her home. Home to my woman.

# CHAPTER
# TWENTY-NINE

## CLEO

It's strange to wake up alone. Since Rage brought me home, I've rarely woken up in bed without him. Furrowing my brows, I remember him coming back to his room and climbing in behind me but neither of us said a word as I drifted back to sleep. Stretching my arms across his pillow to pull it into me, I feel a piece of paper.

Lifting my head, I pick it up to read it.

*Lavender, you were sleeping peacefully and I didn't want to wake you. Had to go on the run this morning. Don't leave the clubhouse and stay inside. Listen to Gadget until I get back, should be late tonight. Love you, be good. ~Travis*

Smiling, I put the note Rage took the time to write on the nightstand right as the need to puke hits again. Rushing to the bathroom, I make it just in time. Ugh, if this part doesn't end soon, I don't know what I'm gonna do.

When the feeling subsides, I get up, brush my teeth, and change into a pair of yoga pants and put on one of Rage's long sleeve shirt. I'm still curious as to why we'd had to come to the clubhouse so early. It's kinda frustrating to be kept in the dark.

Does it have anything to do with my stalker? Or with whatever's going on with the club? Another thing which is frustrating me is the fact I can't have any coffee. Sure, they say one cup is okay but honestly, I'm not taking any chances. I'll settle for a hot cup of tea with honey in it.

Stepping out of the room, I make my way to the main room, stopping at the sight before me. Blinking, I take in all the electronics set up. *Holy mother grail of nerd orgasms.* That's a lot of computer screens. Sitting in the middle of all of them is none other than Gadget, staring at the different monitors.

"Morning," Gadget calls out never once taking his eyes off the screens in front of him.

"Morning," I grumble finally stepping out of my stupor. "Why does it look like you've transformed this room into something you'd find in Iron Man's basement?"

Gadget burst out laughing. "I'll take that as a compliment for my system. Granted, I don't have shit on Tony Stark. Man's a fuckin' genius," he chuckles.

"Well, if Tony were here, he'd be impressed. Why do you have it all set up out here?" I ask making my way toward the bar so I can grab a mug and heat some water in the microwave.

"Need to be able to see what's on the cameras and be in here with you beautiful ladies," Gadget responds.

"Beautiful ladies?" I lift my head, grinning at him.

"Yeah, darlin', you, Lynsdey, Izzy, and Kenny," Gadget says, his brows furrowing together as he pulls out his phone. Shaking my head, I go back to fixing my tea.

"Morning," Izzy calls out as she enters the main room heading in my direction. She has a hand placed on her stomach, wincing as she rounds the bar to grab her a coffee cup. "I swear this kid is gonna end up kicking me hard enough I pee on myself."

"I have to agree with you. JC would kick but never like this one. He or she has decided my bladder is their trampoline," Kenny grumbles right behind her.

"Oh, I don't want to hear it you two. I carried two and didn't pee myself when they decided to do somersaults," Lynsdey says, carrying two infant car seats. Lifting a brow in question at the sight. "It's easier to put them in their car seats to carry them around together when I'm by myself. They're both still so small, I don't want to take the chance of ever dropping them," she says almost embarrassed to admit her fears.

"There's nothing wrong with the way you put them in their car seats. One baby is hard enough by themselves, add another one, it's twice the work," Gadget speaks up, having been eavesdropping.

"Thanks, Gadget, any word when the guys will be back? I have things that need to be done and don't have time to be on lockdown," Lynsdey says. I quietly keep my thoughts of lockdown to myself as my friends begin to go on about how there is still so much to do before the charity event and none of us have time to be sitting around here twiddling our thumbs like a bunch of old woman in a nursing home. I, for one, am not complaining, considering the threat hanging over my head.

A knock at the door interrupts us. Weird, no one ever knocks on the door. It's always unlocked. "Do me a favor ladies, move to the hallway with the bedrooms in it." Gadget orders, standing from his geek station and moving for the door. The four of us hurry to do as he says. I pick up one of the carriers to help make it easier for Lynsdey.

From the mouth of the hallway, we all try to hear what's being said but other than understanding a handful of curses, we can't make anything out. When Gadget comes into view, fury rolls off him. "Listen up, it's only me here with the prospects, so what I'm about to tell you to do, do it without question. Got me?" Gadgets words send a shiver down my spine. Nodding, we go down the hall and he puts us all in one of the rooms together. "Now, don't leave this room no matter what you hear," he growls, closing the door behind him.

"What the hell is going on that he would order us to stay in here?" Lynsdey whispers, rocking her babies.

"I don't know much other than Twister telling me shit was getting heated with the Dragons Fire MC and we'd be put on lockdown," Izzy says.

We all sit, silently waiting for Gadget to come back. Gunfire can be heard from where we are, then silence again. Oh god no — Gadget. Please let him be okay. Where are the rest of the guys when we need them? What about the prospects?

"Come out, come out, wherever you are? Cleo, I know you're here somewhere," a distorted voice calls out. All three of my friends turn to me with wide eyes. They know me almost as well as Rage does, if not better. So of course, when I move to stand, they try to stop me. "If you don't show yourself, I'll be sure to kill not only your friends but their children as well," the voice calls out yet again.

"I can't let them kill you all. Please tell Rage I love him." Tears fall down my cheeks as I move to the door. Turning the knob, I step out as quietly as I can.

"There you are, bitch." The person turns to face me at the sound of the door closing. "Get over here, it's time for you to pay what's due to me." They snatch my arm tight in a grip I'm sure will leave a bruise. At the moment, I'm sure a bruise is the last thing I need to worry about. Dragging me through the main room, I spot Gadget and Ace on the floor bleeding. A gasp escapes me at the sight.

"I told that man of yours he couldn't keep you from me." Stepping outside, I get a good look at the person. They're covered head to toe but it has to be a woman, but who? Cristy? The only part of them I can see is their eyes and they don't look the same. Color contacts maybe?

"Move your ass, bitch, I ain't got all day. Those dumbasses could be back any minute." Shoving me forward, they point a gun at me. "No funny business. Head toward the tree line."

Once at the tree line, I spot a Polaris Ranger ATV waiting for us. I stop reluctantly— further in the distance, I can hear motorcycles coming our way. If I can prolong enough, I might be able to hold this crazy lunatic off. My plan is stopped by the gun she puts to my head.

"Don't even think about it," she screeches.

"Please, let me go. I haven't done anyt—" Pain explodes in my head from the force of her hitting the side of my face with the gun.

"You've done everything. Now, get the fuck in before I kill you right here, leaving your body for them to find in their own backyard. I want to have my fun first, so move."

I do as she says, getting in the passenger side. My face hurts from the hit to my cheek. Reaching up, I touch it and pulling back, I see blood. She must have cut my cheek.

"You're gonna take a little nap. Don't want to spoil the fun before we get there," she says. I barely look at her when the gun comes down on my head. My vision blurs, then she does it again and all I see is darkness.

# CHAPTER THIRTY

## RAGE

By the time I get to the clubhouse, exhaustion has me draggin'. I can barely keep myself upright due to the blood loss. The parking lot doesn't seem right. Ace, who'd been ordered to stand at the front door, is missing.

Shooting a look to the others, I get off my bike and stalk toward the door, pulling my gun out as I go. Opening the door, I stop in my tracks seeing Gadget and Ace on the floor surrounded by blood. Ice fills my veins and I forget about the blood loss. I rush for Ace as Dragon goes to his twin.

Putting a finger to Ace's throat, I drop my head— he's gone. Motherfucker, whoever did this is gonna regret it. He was a good dude, who would've made a good brother to the club.

Looking over to Dragon, I see him putting pressure to Gadget's wound.

"Call an ambulance," he growls out, not taking his eyes off his brother.

"Already on it, man," Burner states.

"The girls," I state. Moving down the hall, I call out for them, waiting for them to answer me. One of the doors opens and Kenny, Izzy, and Lynsdey all come out sobbing, holding on to each other.

"Where's Cleo?" I bite out, not meaning to sound harsh but my woman is missing.

"Th . . . The . . . They took her," Izzy sobs barely able to get the words out.

"How long ago?" I ask more gently this time.

"Maybe five, ten minutes ago. I'm not sure. Sh . . . She didn't want to go but whoever it was threatened to kill the kids and she refused to listen."

My breathing picks up as I take in Izzy's words. Fuck. Fuck. Motherfuckin' fuck. It's gotta be her stalker who got to her. And of course, my woman would go to protect these children. She wouldn't see a child hurt because of her. Damnit. I hang my head in shame— I failed her yet again.

I need to get a grip on the fury beginning to swirl around me. "Alright, I want you three to take the kids either back in the room you were in or one of your rooms and stay there. Watch a movie and let me and the rest of the guys handle shit out here," I tell them turning to move back to the main room. I can hear the sirens coming now. Thank fuck.

Minutes later, the room is swarming with officers and medics. Police begin to question us while the medics work to save Gadget. Ace was pronounced DOA.

"Sir, you're bleeding. We need to get you checked out," one of the medics says, coming toward me.

"You can go help your buddies with Gadget, he's more important. I'll live," I growl in his face.

"We need to call the Prez, get the club back here fuckin' quick," Hades says quietly enough no one besides us hears him.

"Do we know who did this?" Dragon growls, staring at the medics.

"It better not have been the Dragons Fire," Burner grinds out through his teeth.

"It wasn't them, Cleo's missing. We need to get the pigs out of here soon. I need to find my woman. The longer they take, the longer it will take me to find her," I growl and all three sets of eyes turn in my direction.

"The other girls and kids are okay?" Hades asks.

"Yeah, told them to go watch a movie and stay there for now," I say turning my attention to the pig walking my way.

"Good," Hades mutters under his breath.

"We're about wrapped up here since you guys don't have any answers for us, and have stated no one else was here," the pig states eyeing the three of us before zeroing in on the wound on my chest. I should've probably put a shirt on but right now, I couldn't give a rat's ass about it. "That being said, if you do think of something give me a call," he hands me the card.

"Dragon, why don't you round up the women and take them with you to the hospital," I suggest knowing he won't be able to focus with Gadget in the state he's in. He snaps his eyes over to me asking with his eyes if I'm sure. Nodding my head, "Yeah man, we need someone at the hospital with him and you can take the girls. I know they're probably in whichever room pissed at not knowing."

I wait for them to load up Gadget in one ambulance and put Ace's body in the back of a coroner's van. They must've been called in after they called it. Glancing around the room, a thought occurs to me. Fuck.

"I just realized something, brothers. Where's the new prospect and Shadow?" I ask. Rushing toward the back of the club, we find no one there.

"Rage, look at the ground over here," Hades calls out. Moving to him, I check out what he's talking about. Seeing it, I narrow my eyes as I follow the tracks. From the looks of it, someone was being dragged through here.

Following the drag marks, they stop at the shed. Pulling out my gun, I open the door enough to glance inside. "Fuck, found Shadow," I say, moving to his side to check his pulse. I blow out a breath finding it steady. Whoever got him only knocked him out cold.

"One of y'all stay with him. I'm goin' huntin'," I state, moving toward the entrance to the shed. Now I need to focus on the one thing that matters most to me— finding my woman and bringing her home.

"I'm coming for you, Lave, just hang on for me," I murmur to the sky. Turning my head toward Burner, I give him a nod. "Let's go fuck some people up. It's time this lunatic learned you don't fuck with the DRMC," I growl out letting the rage I'm known for take hold.

*No one fucks with my family.*

# CHAPTER THIRTY-ONE

## CLEO

"Time to wake up, bitch," a female voice says as she slaps me across the face. Groaning, I try to bring my hand up to rub my cheek only to realize both hands are restrained behind my back. I open my eyes and at first, it's blurry, thanks to the woman standing in front of me.

When my vision clears, I get my first real look at her. She looks familiar, however, I can't place where I know her from. She could be classified as stunning with a tiny figure if she wasn't glaring down at me with animosity in her eyes. Taking her in some more, I notice she has her hair almost like mine, almost as if she were trying to mimic me. She even seems to dress the way I usually do. Which isn't too off, well except for how she has her hair. With the way she's made her appearance, she really could be my twin if not my sibling and no one would question it. The only difference is our eyes and the fact I have bigger boobs.

Turning my head slowly, I recognize the room I'm in, panic begins to hit me. We're in Lynsdey's childhood house. Lynsdey put this place up for sale the moment she could. She didn't want anything to do with her past and the horrors that came with it.

"Who are you?" I finally ask.

"Really, you don't know?" she says, almost looking hurt. "Of course, you don't, considering the fact that I've always been in the shadows compared to you," she grinds out, pacing and mumbling under breath, sending me malicious glares. Furrowing my brows, I don't get it. What does she mean she's always been in the shadows compared to me?

"I'm sorry, I don't know who you are," I try again, unable to figure out how I know this woman. With her looking almost identical to myself, you'd think I'd know her.

"Oh, you're gonna be sorry, bitch. It's because of you I've lost everything," she screeches. Footsteps above us draw her attention away from me. I watch as she walks toward the door. Opening it, she yells out to whoever it is up there to bring her toy down. Shivers run down my spine as memories of words similar to those run through my head.

When she comes back toward me, she has an evil glint in her eyes I've seen before. I feel my face growing pale as memories form with the present. Shaking my head to clear it, I try to alleviate it of things that can't happen anymore— he's dead.

"Now, I'm gonna tell you a little story while I wait for my toy to be brought to me. Maybe then, you will know who I am," she announces as she goes back to pacing. "Several years ago, I fell in love with the most amazing man. Granted, he didn't know at first. I watched him from afar, admiring everything about him. He was absolutely beautiful, even when he was doing horrible things. Then he saw you, and you took him from me. I'd planned to show him how much I loved him, that I didn't care if he did what he did but of course, when he saw you, he made *you* his. Not me," she screeches out the last part as she slaps me across the face again.

My stomach turns at the realization she's talking about Jake. "Then you and that bitch of a stepsister had to go and put him away. I was pissed at first, thought about going after both of you then. But I sent him a letter one day, professing my love to him and that I'd be waiting for him until he was released. When he replied, it was like the beginning of us. He'd told me how sorry he was for not being with me. Said when he came home, we could be together. I was so happy to get what I wanted. Then you two bitches had to ruin it all again and get him killed by those bikers." Her voice is filled with venom on the last part. "I planned to seek my revenge out on you both, however, I figured with Lynsdey being with one of those bikers, it would be easier to get to you. I mean you were the one I really wanted anyway. Thinking you can have whatever you want. Even Cristy's man."

The sound of the door to the basement opening causes her to smile. "Oh good, Darren is bringing me my toy," she says with glee as a man drags a woman behind him. One look at the man and my eyes widen. It's the new prospect from the club. He slings the woman down on the floor at my stalker's feet.

"Here you go, Megs, need anything else?" Darren asks slurring his words.

"No, I'm good here, thank you for bringing me my toy," she says, patting Darren on the arm. "Now go on upstairs. I'll be up later and give you another dose."

Darren doesn't even look my way or at the other woman as he turns to leave the room.

"Please Megan, let me go." The whimper of the woman on the floor draws my attention her way. I gasp at the realization it's Cristy. Scanning over her body, welts cover her skin where she's not covered by the small tank top and underwear.

"Shut up, Cristy, you brought this on yourself just like Cleo did," Megan yells, kicking Cristy in the stomach. "Now, let me finish the rest of my story. You see, when I got hired at Outlaw Rack's, I instantly made friends with Cristy and we started talking about how she wanted Rage and told me she'd planned to make her move shortly after you left. Figured she could help him get over you. But he wouldn't give her the time of day." That's when it clicks, I'd seen her working at the bar. She'd been one of the new waitresses Kenny hired.

"I'm sorry, Cleo, I didn't mean for this all to hap—" Cristy screams at the impact of Megan kicking her again.

"Shut up, bitch," Megan screams. Leaning down, she grabs Cristy by the hair. "Speak out like that again, my toy, and I'll prolong my fun with you," she says, kissing her hard on the mouth. "Mhmm, and you know how I do love to keep the fun going." Oh, God, it's like watching my past come to life with a female version of Jake.

"You do know I didn't take everything from you. I didn't want Jake. He was delusional and a rapist," I finally speak up earning Megan's wrath.

"Don't you start with your lies, bitch. He told me all about how you wanted it. Just like all those other women, and they deserved everything they got," Megan screams out clenching her hair in her hands, pulling it. "You know when you came back, I thought I might be able to stand you being here but then I saw how you were treated that night you came to the bar with Izzy. Men gawked at you like you were the hottest piece of ass. I knew then you needed to either leave again, which I was willing to let happen, considering I wanted nothing more than to kill you. But you refused to leave so I have no choice but to do to you as those men did to Jake."

Well, fuck a monkey's ass and let pigs shit gold, this bitch needs to be in the looney bin. I hope like hell I can either figure a way out of here or someone finds me. One thing is for sure, I refuse to let this lunatic win. I will not be a victim again.

# CHAPTER THIRTY-TWO

## RAGE

Hours pass as I track the tree line. From what the girls told me, I figured whoever took my woman didn't use the road. We would have seen them go past that way on our way here. Took me about an hour to find what I was looking for— track marks. Burner and I began tracking the marks through the woods when we hear the rumbling of bikes coming down the road.

"The rest of the brothers must be back," Burner states keeping his eyes on the tire tracks on the ground.

"Yeah, let's head back in for a minute to get an update. I ain't got all day to find my woman, times tickin'. We don't know what this lunatic could be doing to Cleo," I growl turning to head toward the clubhouse.

The instant Twister spots me and Burner coming out of the trees, he rushes our way. "What the fuck happened here?" Twister roars out as he gets closer. He's pissed and I can't blame him for it.

"Where's my woman and kids?" Thorn growls out from next to him.

I hold my hand up to stop any more questions from them, I

know they all want answers and to see their women. "You must not have checked your phones. We sent you a message to let you know we had an emergency here. When we got here, we walked into the club to find Gadget and Ace on the floor surrounded in blood. Dragon and your women went to the hospital to be with Gadget. The last update, he was heading straight to surgery. Ace was DOA when we got here. Cleo's missing." I growl out the last part.

"Fuck, Ace's dead, Gadget's in surgery, and Cleo's missing," Twister mutters under his breath. "What about Shadow and Darren?" he asks.

"Shadows okay, we found him knocked out in the shed, still can't find Darren. Right now, he's the least of my concern. I need to find Cleo. There're tire tracks back in the woods starting right in the tree line. Whoever this lunatic is, had the sense to stay off the main road. With that being said, they could've taken my woman anywhere. We need to see the feed from the cameras to see if we got this person on video," I say impatiently.

"Alright, let's go check the security system, then we need to figure out a game plan," Twister says, turning to head inside. I don't bother warning him that it's not a pretty sight inside. He can see for himself.

Stepping inside the clubhouse, my brothers' curses can be heard. I don't bother to pay attention to them having already seen the worst of it. They at least didn't have to see their brothers laying on that floor the way we did when we got here.

Heading toward where Gadget had his system set up, I pull up the video stream from earlier. Scanning through, I stop at the motion of Ace banging against the outside of the door. Glancing at the inside camera, I watch as Gadget orders the women to move to the hallway. Going to the door, he speaks to Ace for a moment. His face becomes a mask of anger as he closes the door again. Moving to the hallway, he moves the women to a room further down the hall, the same one they were in when I called out to them. Moving to another screen, I see a blacked-out figure moving toward the back of the clubhouse, walking straight to Darren. I can't make out the words exchanged between the two of them before they both turn to come into the clubhouse.

Switching to the one with Ace again, he's standing there doing as he's supposed to all the way up until Darren shoots him. Ace's body jerks. He quickly steps inside the door, leaving Darren and the blacked-out figure outside, moving in the direction of the door. Right outside the door, the figure looks up at the camera, their eyes are filled with malice as they step through.

Turning back to the inside video feed, my head is spinning from all the back and forth. How does Gadget fuckin' do this? My stomach turns seeing everything play out in front of me. The audio on the inside is better. Gadget is pulling his gun out as Ace falls to the floor holding a hand to his stomach when the other two come in shooting. Fuck, he didn't even have a chance to pull the trigger on these fuckers. When we get our hands on Darren, he's dead.

"Trick or treat dumbasses," the figures distorted laughter fills the room as she steps over Ace's body. "Darren, go make sure the other prospect is taken care of while I get Cleo, she's nothing I can't handle, stupid bitch." At those words, I don't finish the video, I can't. If I do, I will see just how much of a failure I am to Cleo and our child.

"Motherfucker," I roar out slamming my fist into the wall behind me. You'd think the pain from the wound in my shoulder and now the pain in my hand would be enough to stop me. It doesn't. "Prez, why don't you all go up to the hospital and check on your women, me a few others can handle tracking this dumbass down."

"Not happenin', brother, we do this together. Cleo is just as important to the rest of us as the other women. Plus, they'd have our balls if we didn't stay here to help. Now, let's figure out where she is," Twister says sternly.

"Hades, you know how to check the tracking devices that are in all the phones? We find Darren, we might just find Cleo," Horse suggests.

"Yeah, give me a minute. I may not be as tech-savvy as Gadget but I can get around," Hades grumbles moving to the computer. Minutes later, he has the location of Darren's phone, dumbass never ditched it— which is a small stroke of luck for us.

"Come on, brothers, strap up with whatever you need and let's go," Twister orders turning his attention to me. "Rage, I swear we're gonna get her back, nothing is gonna happen to her or that baby she's carrying."

"I hear ya, Prez, but I won't be able to believe your words until I have my woman back in my arms," I say moving toward the door. As this lunatic told me the other day, it's time for them to pay what's due.

# CHAPTER THIRTY-THREE

## CLEO

After Megan finishes spewing of what she has planned, she turns her attention from me to Cristy. Making me endure watching everything sexual along with the torture she does to the woman who I use to call my friend.

"Please stop, Megan, please, I can't take it anymore." Cristy's whimpers fill the room.

"But you're so much fun to play with." Megan laughs like a lunatic. How no one ever noticed the crazy in her, I don't know. This woman is like a female version of Chucky. And not his bride either. Tiffany's psychotic but she's a dumb bitch compared to Chucky.

A loud knock at the top of the stairs draws Megan's attention from Cristy for a split second. "Don't think about goin' anywhere, Cristy. I'll be right back, then we'll have some more fun," she says, her eyes sliding between the two of us.

Neither of us makes a sound as Megan goes up the stairs. Listening to the murmurs of Megan and Darren speaking quietly, I wiggle my hands. I've been doing this a bit to try and loosen the rope. My wrists have become sore from rubbing against it. It doesn't matter as long as I can get loose. I know if I don't take my chance now, this is it for me. Maybe if Cristy is willing to help, I can get us both out of here.

"Cristy, look, I know you hate me but untie me and we can get out of here," I tell her hoping she listens.

"How are you gonna get us out of here? Megan is an evil bitch incarnate," Cristy sneers.

"Don't be a fuckin' bitch about it. Untie my hands and I'll show you. Now, hurry up so we can get out of here," I whisper yell to get her to listen. God damn, pig snottin' bitches and not listening. I've been in this situation, I don't want to go through it again. All I need her to do is untie my freaking hands and I'll do the rest.

"Fine, but if we get caught, I'm telling her it's all your fault," Cristy says sarcastically, sounding like a damn teenager not getting their way with their parents. Was she always like this? Honestly, I'm not sure. I'd like to think we'd been good friends but, in all reality, I don't think we were.

Soon as she has my hands loosened enough, I pull my wrist free. Sharp stinging sensation courses through my hands as I move them to get some blood flow to them. Standing up, I grab the chair and move toward the window I knew was down here, the same one Lynsdey used to escape Jake. Ironic really that her and I both having to escape from her childhood home.

"Come on, we're going out this window. Soon as you're out, head for the trees straight ahead," I tell Cristy as I place the chair right under the window. I let her go out first, knowing she's in a weaker state than I am considering all she'd been through. Nodding her head, she climbs up the chair, opens the window and slides through. It's a tight space but we're both small enough to fit through. Even with my big boobs, I know I can make it.

Once she's through the window, I move to do the same. Only a hand grabs my ankle causing me to scream out trying to pull me back inside. "You stupid cunt, how dare you try to fuckin' escape," Megan screams. Kicking out, I use all my strength which isn't much since I'm hanging halfway out the window. Finally, I get loose and the rest of the way out the window. Standing up, I make a run for the trees, hoping to get as far away from her as I can.

Sprinting through the woods, I spot Cristy not far ahead of me as I move to catch up to her. She's moving a lot slower than she should be. Reaching her, I grab hold of her hand, dragging her with me.

"I don't know if I can keep up," Cristy breaths out.

"Cristy, you have to, if not Megan is gonna catch you and who the hell knows what she will do then. We just need to make it a little further, come on," I whisper as I continue to keep my pace.

A gun firing from behind me causes me to release Cristy's hand. Turning, I find Megan barreling down on us.

"Run," I scream at Cristy as I retake her hand dragging her with me.

"I can't, I just can't," Cristy cries out as she stumbles forward. I try to help her regain her footing, but she ends up taking both of us to the ground.

"I swear to fuckin' God, I don't know what everyone sees in you," Megan says, coming to stand over the both of us. "Cristy, I'm disappointed. You complained and complained about how Cleo came back and took what you wanted. You're pathetic."

"I'm done having fun with you," Megan says calmly as she lifts her gun, aiming it right at Cristy's head. I scream out as she fires. I'm frozen in place, staring at Cristy's lifeless face. Blood oozing from the hole between her eyes.

"Why?" I ask finally looking at Megan again. She's glaring at me as if annoyed at my question.

"I've already told you why, sweet Cleo. Without you here, I can finally have everything that I've ever wanted. Well, not everything since you had my man killed. You know, maybe I'll go back to the clubhouse and kill Rage, see if you can understand the way it feels to lose someone," she laughs like killing my husband is funny to her.

"Look, Megan, I didn't even know who you were before today. How could I take something from someone I didn't even know?" I say trying to distract her in order to maybe get to where I can make a run for it or attempt to get the gun from her.

"You didn't know who I was," she mutters to herself then screams it at the top of her lungs waving her gun haphazardly in my direction. "Bitch, I've known who you were since we were in high school and ever since you have done nothing but ruin my life. You should know exactly who I am. I've already told you this," she says. "You know, it's funny how things come to an end. These woods are where you caught Jake's eye and these woods are where you're gonna pay the price of takin' his life. Goodbye, bitch," she says, aiming the gun in my direction. I turn to make a run for it, feeling a sharp pain in my leg. Screaming out, I fall sideways on the ground hoping the impact doesn't hurt the baby.

I'm trying hard to get back up when Megan's foot presses into my back, pushing me into the ground. "I missed on purpose you know," she says, grinding down on the middle of my back.

Before I can say another word, Megan is pulled off of me, kicking and screaming.

"Lavender, baby, I got you," Rage says, kneeling on the ground next to me.

"I knew you'd come for me," I murmur, exhausted from the day's events. "I think you need to get me to the hospital though. I'm bleeding and my face hurts."

"You got it, Lave," he says, lifting me up to cradle me in his arms.

"What do you want to do with this bitch?" one of the guys calls out.

"I say bury her ass alive, let her suffocate to death," Burner says, his voice full of anger.

"No, please, don't. That's too kind for her," I say softly. All eyes turn to me. "What?" I ask.

"What would you suggest we do to her?" Twister asks, stepping closer to Rage and I. Looking up at Rage, seeing the rage and anger swirling in his eyes, I know exactly what I'd do to her.

"I say we tie her to Lynsdey's childhood home and light the night up with her flames. Let the fire begin with her and end with the house burned to a crisp. Then Lynsdey's and my nightmares can finally end," I tell Twister. His eyes widen then soften as it dawns on him and probably everyone else around us this is where it all began.

"Would you like to do the honors of lighting the match?" he asks.

"No. I think Rage and Thorn should get that honor. Actually, I think every member of the club here should have the honor with all she's done." Tears fill my eyes as I remember Gadget on the floor. "Please tell me Gadget is okay," I say looking up at Rage then the rest of the guys around us.

Sorrow fills the air. "Yeah, Lavender, he was alive last time we checked. He's in surgery. Though I should tell you Ace is gone."

I put my face to his chest as I sob for all that's happened. "I'm sorry, Travis," I whisper.

"Don't be sorry, come on, let's get you out of here and checked. Need to be sure you and our baby are both good. They can light the sky up without me. You're more important," Rage says, turning and heading through the woods.

Relaxing in his arms, I nod in agreement. I need to be sure our baby is safe and sound.

# CHAPTER THIRTY-FOUR

## RAGE

Pride fills me at Cleo's words replaying in my head. I've been sitting here next to her as she sleeps. I refused to let the nurses or doctors tend to my shoulder. I don't want to leave her side. Doctor Longsten came to see her and ordered an ultrasound. I let out a relieved breath seeing our child with a strong, steady heartbeat just like it should be.

"Rage," Cleo's voice draws my attention to her face. Her cheek is swollen and bruised, the doctor said they'd be keeping her here overnight for observation.

"Yeah, baby," I say, moving closer to her.

"Will you please go get that shoulder looked at and the other two wounds you have?" she whispers.

"I'm not leaving your side, baby. Not this time," I tell her.

"Then get Doctor Connors in here. You need to have it looked at," she says, glaring at me.

Chuckling, I give her what she wants by hitting the call button on the side of the bed. When the nurse comes in, I ask if she can page Doctor Connors for us. Moments later, she walks into Cleo's room carrying a tray of instruments in her hand and Dragon right behind her.

"About time you had me paged. Dragon had already informed me of the bullet lodged in your shoulder. Now, usually, we do this differently, but I know you're stubborn and will refuse to do this the right way," she says, putting the tray down and getting right to it.

No one in the room says anything as she goes about getting the area cleaned up and numb. I clench my teeth together as she reaches in, pulling the bullet out. "You're lucky it didn't get embedded in your shoulder. I'm gonna stitch this up, then we'll move on to the other two," Doctor Connors says sternly. I don't respond to her comments. "If I give you a sling, are you gonna wear it?" Doctor Connors asks when she's done and throwing her gloves away.

"Doctor Connors, I'll make sure he wears it," Cleo says, speaking up before I can answer her with a flat-out no. Looking toward my woman, I lift a brow at her statement. "Oh, you'll wear the sling if you want to have sex with me again," she threatens, crossing her arms over her chest.

"Well, I'll bring a sling in here and I suggest you listen to Cleo," Doctor Connors says, walking out of the room.

"You're gonna have your hands full with that one, Dragon." I chuckle at the glower he throws my way.

"Don't remind me," he grumbles, leaving to follow his doctor like a dragon needing to protect its treasure.

"How's Gadget?" Cleo asks quietly. Since being here, she hasn't been able to be updated on him.

"Lave, he's in critical condition right now. They've placed him in a coma, for now, to help him heal. The bullet missed his heart by centimeters. We almost lost him but he's a fighter and will get through this."

"That's good he will be okay," she whispers sucking in a breath. "I feel like this is all my fault." She looks at me.

"Not your fault, Lavender, never take this on your shoulders. Leave it where it belongs with that lunatic woman who thought the world should circle around her," I tell her gently. "How about I send one of the guys to get you some Chinese food? You need to keep up your strength," I suggest.

Hitching her breath, she smiles. "That would be great. Can I have chicken lo mein and General Tso? Oh, and some egg rolls with duck sauce," she asks sweetly.

"You got it, baby," I say, pulling my phone out, shooting a text off to Burner.

"Thank you," she says, her eyes drooping. Not even a minute later, my woman is sound asleep.

---

"You've got to be kidding me, Rage. You can't be out here working on your bike when you're supposed to be keeping that arm in a sling." Her voice yells out from just inside the door of the house. We've been home for two days and she refuses to listen when I tell her to rest.

Chuckling, I put the wrench down on the ground next to my bike. "Babe, seriously, you're one to talk. You've been moving around the house like you're not supposed to be in bed resting. When you do as your told, I'll wear the fuckin' sling," I growl out, moving toward her.

Huffing, she turns to go back inside but the crutches she needs to get around catch on the door frame and she begins to stumble. She barely stops herself from falling to the ground.

Running the rest of the way to her, I lift her into my arms, carrying her ass back in the house, sitting her on the couch. "Baby, if you don't take it easy, I'll end up having to wear that ass of yours out," I growl into her ear.

"Oh please, you're not gonna do anything to my ass," she giggles.

"Oh, you wanna bet? Let's see about that why don't we," I murmur laying her flat on the couch.

Placing a knee gently between her legs, doing my best to avoid her injured one, I lean forward to take her mouth. Kissing her deeply, I run my hands along her sides, cupping her tits. God, I fuckin' love them. With the top she's wear, I am easily able to pull it down. Taking one nipple in my mouth, I suck it deeply while pinching her other nipple between my fingers.

"Oh, God, Travis," she moans, putting her hands in my hair.

Groaning, I switch to her other breast, giving it the same attention with my tongue, loving the feel of her pulling my hair. Needing to be inside her, I slide her pants down, taking her underwear with them to her thighs. Standing, I pull my pants down far enough to pull my dick out— he's already hard and ready to go. Lifting her legs, I slam deep inside her in one thrust. Her screams of pleasure spur me on. I fuck her fast and hard, bringing her to two orgasms before finally finding my own. I come deep inside her pussy, calling out her name.

"Damn, that was good," I groan, barely holding myself over her.

"You got that right, now can we just lay here and snuggle for the rest of the day," she whispers.

"Whatever you want, Lavender," I murmur against her ear, placing a kiss to it.

"Thank you, Travis," she says.

"Why are you thanking me, babe?" I ask her.

"For giving me the family I always wanted," she says, smiling up at me.

"Lave, it should be me thanking you. You brought life back into me the moment I laid eyes on you," I say, kissing her.

And I mean every word of it— she's the life I need in this world. I'll do everything in my power to keep her with me. She's my beautiful Lavender that brings peace to my soul.

# EPILOGUE

## CLEO

"There's no way I'm going out on that stage," I grumble. It's the night of the concert and the girls have been great about leaving me alone about it. However, they don't seem to realize I don't want to sing in front of a huge ass crowd of people even if it's for charity.

"Oh, don't be a baby, just two songs and you can be done. It's for charity, Cleo, come on," Izzy says, moving around the room, her hand sitting on her stomach. It seems to have doubled in size over the last few weeks. I smile thinking about my own baby resting soundly inside me. I can't wait to experience everything I thought I wouldn't.

"Ugh, fine, two songs and no more okay," I say, huffing.

"Yay! Great, thank you, now let's get you out there, you're up first," Izzy says, smiling.

"Wait, what?" I ask, confused.

"Oh, please, like I'd have given you time to back out of this. You have an amazing voice and I'm honored to have you singing the songs we picked out," Izzy's voice wobbles on the last part of her sentence. She struggled with so much after losing her brother and I must admit, being a part of this event fills me with joy. She's honoring his life by helping children who have lost a parent.

Sighing, I take a steady breath. "Okay, let's get out there then," I say, moving toward the door. I've only been without crutches for two days now and even though my leg is still sore from it being shot, I can at least walk on it now.

My hands are shaking as I walk out on the stage. Looking out to the crowd, I instantly find Rage, front and center, watching me. He smiles, nodding his head letting me know I can do this. I'd been telling him all week I didn't want to be on stage, in the spotlight. I'd confided in him about everything Megan said. Rage listened, letting me get it all out, then processed to explain things differently. Telling me it wasn't my fault her life was shit and that she needed to put blame on someone else. Sucks it had to be me and a small part of me feels sorry for her. Then again, I know she ended up getting what she deserved. As she said, it should end where it all began.

When Lynsdey found out the house was burned to the ground, she didn't shed one single tear. In fact, she sighed in relief. That house held so many nightmares for both of us. Now, she and I can leave the past just as it should be, behind us.

Shaking my thoughts, I give Rage a small wave as I move further onto the stage. Chaz comes out carrying a stool and placing it next to me. "Have a seat, sweetheart. Rage ordered us to have this for you," he laughs, nodding in Rage's direction. Turning my head, I blow Rage a kiss.

"Alright, ladies and gentlemen, you all know us as Demons Among Us and we're here to play tonight to honor those who have lost a loved one. Now, the charity was created to help bring peace to children who have lost a parent. But tonight, we're playing to honor those who are no longer with us, whether it be a child you never met, a sibling, spouse, or parent. Please know you're not alone in this world," Chaz announces to the crowd. "Now, let's give it up to Cleo as she joins the band for a few songs."

The crowd cheers as Hunter begins to strum his guitar. Tanner follows on his bass and Lex with the drums. Chaz cues me when to begin. Closing my eyes, I envision the words in my mind. Opening my mouth, I begin to sing, *'Every Little Thing'* by Carly Pearce. When the song ends, I open my eyes and find Rage, letting him center me right as the next song begins. Keeping my eyes on him, I sing *'Bring on the Rain'* directly to him.

At the end of the song, I walk to the edge of the stage where he meets me, taking me in his arms and holding me close—right where I want to be for the rest of my life.

*Be sure to follow or stalk me!*

Goodreads
Bookbub
DRMC BABES
Instagram
Author Page

## ALSO BY E.C. LAND

**Devil's Riot MC**

Horse's Bride

Thorn's Revenge

Twister's Survival

Reclaimed (Devil's Riot MC Boxset Bks 1 – 3)

Cleo's Rage

Connors' Devils

Hades Pain

Badger's Claim

Burner's Absolution

Redeemed (Devil's Riot MC Boxset Bks 4 – 6)

K-9's Fight

Revived Boxset (Devil's Riot MC Boxset Bks 7 — 9)

Red's Calm

**Devil's Riot MC Originals**

Stoney's Property

Owning Victoria

Blaze's Mark

Taming Coyote

Luna's Shadow

Choosing Nerd

Ranger's Fury

Carrying Blaze's Mark

Neo's Strength

Cane's Dominance

Venom's Prize

Devil's Ride (DRMC Boxset 1-5)

Protecting Blaze's Mark

Whip's Breath

Viper's Touch

**Devil's Riot MC Southeast**

Hammer's Pride

Malice's Soul

Axe's Devotion

Rebelling Rogue

Ruin Boxset 1-3

Remaining Gunner's

**Devil's Riot MC Tennessee**

Blow's Smoke

**Inferno's Clutch MC**

Chains' Trust

Breaker's Fuse

Ryder's Rush

Axel's Promise

Fated for Pitch Black

Tiny's Hope

Their Redemption Boxset 1 - 5

Fuse's Hold

Nora's Outrage

Tyres' Wraith

Brielle's Nightmare

Pipe's Burn

Their Salvation Boxset 6 - 10

**Dark Lullabies**

A Demon's Sorrow

A Demon's Bliss

A Demon's Harmony

A Demon's Soul

A Demon's Song

Dark Lullabies Boxset

**Royal Bastards MC (Elizabeth City Charter)**

Cyclone of Chaos

Spiral into Chaos

**Aligned Hearts**

Embraced

Entwined

Entangled

Ensnared

Crush Boxset 1-3

Entrapped

**Night's Bliss**

Finley's Adoration (Co-Write with Elizabeth Knox)

Cedric's Ecstasy

Arwen's Rapture

**Satan's Keepers MC**

Keeping Reaper

Forever Tombstone's

Hellhound's Sacrifice

Outrage Boxset 1 - 3

***Toxic Warriors MC***

Viking

Ice

War

**De Luca Crime Family**

Frozen Valentine (Prequel)

Frozen Kiss

**Sons of Norhill Tops**

Inheriting Trouble

**Pins and Needles Series with Elizabeth Knox**

Blood and Agony

Blood and Torment

Blood & Betrayal

Agony Boxset 1 - 3

**DeLancy Crime Family with Elizabeth Knox**

Degrade

Deprave

Detest

Desire Boxset 1 - 3

Deny

Demean

**Raiders of Valhalla with Elizabeth Knox**

Malicious

Sinister

Malevolent

Broken Boxset 1 - 3

Spiteful

Menacing

**Deathstalkers MC with Elizabeth Knox**

Kinetic

***Available on Audible***

Reclaimed

Cleo's Rage

Connors' Devils

Hades Pain

Badger's Claim

**Be sure to check out the first chapter of Horse's Bride in the Reclaimed Boxset. Featuring the first three books in the series.**

Horse's Bride,
Thorns Revenge, & Twister's Survival

**Chapter One**

## HORSE

It's fucking early as hell out, but I can't help that I love the open road, the smell of the fresh air, and the feel of my bike under me as I'm riding. Riding out this morning seeing the sunrise as we make our way out of the national charter's clubhouse lot has to be one of the most amazing sights I've ever seen. Almost as if it were a sign of the things to come as we head towards the new clubhouse that we're expanding.

I feel a calm being out on the open road on my girl, feeling the power she brings me as we make our way on the interstate. Knowing she's the only girl in my life that won't ever fail me no matter the situation we find ourselves in. I can always count on her handling whatever comes our way.

Twister, who is Prez of the Devil's Riot's new charter as well as my best friend, rides next to me heading towards our new location. The brothers had made the decision in our last church session to expand the club with a new charter. Granted there are already several charters up and down the east coast as well as some going towards the Midwest. Our farthest charter is out in Colorado. With us moving to this location it will be the closest charter to any of the docks we deal with. The Russians that we work with are known for dealing in guns and the docks out here are a lot easier to use than most. Less conspicuous. With us moving to the new clubhouse we have fifteen guys and four prospects. Today it's just Twister, Rage, Thorn, and I riding out. The others will be coming tomorrow.

We want to get a good look around and start making a list of all the shit that needs to be done staking out our new territory. Easier to do when it's just four guys instead of the whole club around. When you have a shit ton of brothers walking around the same area it's fucking hard to see everything that needs to get done.

I need gas and to piss, so I signal the Prez by tapping the side my leg to get his attention so he'll pull up to the next gas station we see. He nods as we see a sign for the next station coming on in two miles. Damn, I've been on the road so many times on runs, I've forgotten how bad it is when you've had shit sleep. Lucky for me, cause I really need coffee and aspirin. Twister had wanted to get on the road before dawn this morning so that we can be there before lunch. We had a huge ass bash last night, and the club pussy was thrown our way. Swear all the girls wanted to take a turn with us. I took three of them back to my room, and watched as they took turns sucking me off until I painted their faces with my cum. The fun part was while I had one riding my face, and one on my dick the other would be sucking my nuts or licking her friend's clit. Fuck I've been tired, but never exhausted as I this morning when I got up.

"Why did we have to leave so fucking early again? Couldn't

you have picked a better time to leave than the ass crack of dawn?"

I grumble to Twister as we park our bikes next to the gas pumps. Rage and Thorn both shake their heads, just as tired as I am. Yeah, I'll crash when we get to Twister's sister's house. Not knowing what shape the new clubhouse is in, it makes sense to crash at his sister's for now. All our shit is still back in Stonewall Mills. I'm not going to sleep on the damn floor or pay for a room if I don't have to. Only thing I know about the new clubhouse is that Twister and Stoney, our national Prez, picked it out and had it designed and built for the most part. We're supposed to do the rest. Something tells me there's a lot of clean up. Since all our shit won't be here until later this week when the rest of the guys showed up, we needed a place to crash. No reason to pay for rooms at a motel or sleep on the floor of the clubhouse when his sister lives so close.

Twister turns towards me smirking with a knowing look. "Quit your bitching and shut the fuck up, Horse. You can sleep when you're fucking dead." He says trying to be serious.

I shake my head. "You know I ain't a morning person especially without coffee in my veins."

"Ain't that the fucking truth." He starts laughing. "No fucker, I wanted to head out early so I can surprise my sis with lunch before she heads to work. If I can't catch her before work, I'm hoping to catch her before she gets busy."

Chuckling, I look at him "Why didn't you just say that shit in the first fucking place? Didn't know you were that wrapped around your sister's pinky."

Shaking his head, he grumbles, "I haven't seen her since her birthday a year ago. I've barely had time to talk to her on the phone with all the shit we have going on with the move and all."

Yeah Twister's a sucker for his sister. Never met the chick but I have respect for her from everything that he's said about her. Especially since she's his only blood relative left. The

Bastards Sons took out his dad, and his mom ran out on his sister and him when Twister was seventeen. It left him to take care of his kid sister. His bitch of a mom didn't even bother to explain why she left them, just fucking took off leaving them to fend for themselves. I guess shit moms don't bother explaining though. Twister stepped up big time while prospecting for Devil's Riot. He always made sure his sister was taken care of, being the only male figure in her life. When any of the guys asked about his sister, Twister would go fucking ballistic not wanting anyone to fuck with her, his brothers included.

"So, what's your sister's name anyway?" I ask, fishing for info.

Granted I've never seen her. He doesn't bring her to the club. Evidently, she's been living over four hours away from him for a while now. I wonder why that is. He never brought her around the club before she moved. One day she just up and left without telling her brother.

Twister hangs up the gas pump eyeing me skeptically. "Her name's Kenny."

I freeze. It's an unusual name for a chick and my luck couldn't be that good Or bad.

*Not many girls out there named Kenny though.*

It couldn't be the same girl Kenny was a sweet ass, and I was her first without even realizing it. I can still remember everything about her body.

*Four Years Ago*

*Dammit t, I hate when I gotta go anywhere close to a store that doesn't have anything to do with bike parts. Now that's something I can do but going to the damn grocery store to get shit for the clubhouse? That's a job for the prospects and club whores. I shouldn't be the one going into a damn grocery store. Definitely shouldn't have pissed off the VP last night by trying to hit on his latest piece of ass.*

*Shaking my head as I make my way into the store, I stop dead in my tracks when I spot the hottest body I've ever seen in my life. Tight jeans covering a perfect ass with flip flops and a tank top containing the most gorgeous tits I've ever seen. Across her pale shoulders ran a colored tattoo of two dragons intertwined around each other, extending to each other across her shoulder blades. The best part of the dragons would have to be their eyes: one with an aquamarine color, the other with a ruby tint. Between the two dragons, knelt a naked fairy looking upward at the two of them with her arms extended towards their faces. I liked it at first glance, but seeing it in detail I think it's sick.*

*"That's one wicked-ass tat you got, babe. Where'd you get it done?" I stop behind her, waiting for her to turn around and hoping that her front end matches her back.*

*"Thanks. Ink Masters in Blacksburg," she mumbles, keeping her head down as she scuffles through her purse, not looking up at me like I was hoping she'd do.*

*"No problem. You got a name?" I shoot her another grin while I wait for her to look up at me.*

*"Kenny." She finally turns around and my heart almost comes out of my chest. Her eyes had to be the most spectacular blue I've ever seen. They paired perfectly with the dirty blond hair piled up on her head. She was the most exquisite woman I had ever set my eyes on.*

*"So, how about you and I get out of here and go grab a beer or something." I wouldn't mind getting between those legs of hers instead of having a beer but something about her doesn't make me mind waiting. She looks like she'd be worth it. I can already picture her name spilling off my lips while I drive deep into her.*

*Yep, I could see that happening.*

*She smiles at me with plush lips "Sure, I could use a beer."*

*And I could use that sweet body under me as I come all over those flawless tits. I wonder how have I never seen her before.*

*"Alright, sweet girl let's get moving then."*

That had been the beginning of an impeccable week with Kenny and one that has stuck with me since. Problem is, I still dream of her anytime I fall asleep, no matter if I'm sober or not.

I shake my head, ridding it of the memory that started it all.

It can't be the same chick, it can't be. I can only hope to God that it's not. I know my best friend would kill me if he finds out I touched his sister. It's been unspoken, but we've always known that his sister is off limits. It's club code.

"You ready to get back on the road?" Twister asks. At my nod, he yells out to let the rest of the boys know it's time to get back on the road.

Pulling out of the station and riding next to my Prez and best friend, I feel my mind running a mile a minute. All I can think about is could this be the same Kenny who has been haunting me for the past four years. The woman who I picture every time I fuck some random bitch. The woman that in a week's time, stole my heart and never turned back. The woman I haven't been able to find since I realized she was gone. I swear to fuckin' God if it is, I'll be happy as fuck. I'm also going to be in deep shit.

Made in the USA
Coppell, TX
24 October 2022